At the door, Rebecca looked towards the circle of bright light coming through the porthole window to the theatre and saw figures moving, dressed in theatre green. One figure, taller than the rest, stood with tightly gloved hands in front of him, calm and confident. For a moment she thought he looked at her, but she knew that from the theatre he would see only the round window, and it was steaming up rapidly.

She went out into the darker corridor. He would be gone in six weeks. He would walk out of her life as easily as he had burst into it . . .

Lisa Cooper was brought up on the Isle of Wight and went to a well-known London teaching hospital to train as a nurse. After a short spell as theatre sister, she married an accountant, and their two children also have medical connections, her son being a biologist with a pharmaceutical firm and her daughter a medical scientist in a famous hospital for sick children.

Lisa Cooper feels it is important to show the complete professional integrity of the hero and heroine as well as their deep felt emotions, and she makes a point of carefully researching latest developments in surgery and medical science. Writing as a second career began at home when she was unable to go back to nursing in hospital, and she has now written over thirty books.

LOVE'S HEALING TOUCH

BY

LISA COOPER

MILLS & BOON LIMITED
ETON HOUSE 18–24 PARADISE ROAD
RICHMOND SURREY TW9 1SR

First published in Great Britain 1988 by Mills & Boon Limited

© Lisa Cooper 1988

Australian copyright 1988 Philippine copyright 1988

ISBN 0 263 76042 1

Set in 10 on 12 pt Linotron Times
03–0488–52,000

Photoset by Rowland Phototypesetting Limited Bury St Edmunds, Suffolk Made and printed in Great Britain by William Collins Sons & Co. Limited, Glasgow

CHAPTER ONE

'WHAT's wrong with everyone?' asked Nurse Daphne
Frost with real annoyance.

'With you as well, Daph?' Sister Rebecca Perivale
eyed her staff nurse with amusement. 'Calm down and
tell me the worst. Have they forgotten to collect the
unsterile drums again? Someone didn't bring up the
right dispensary? Or have you seen that I had to change
your off duty?'

'You haven't! Oh, Sister, I need that half day. I have
plans!'

'Not your precious half-day and day off. That's fine,
but we're expecting a bad case as soon as they can get it
here, so we might need you this afternoon.'

'Anything interesting? I'm tired of Dr Weldon's overweight hypochondriacs.' Daphne Frost bit her lip as she
saw the faint flush mounting on the usually porcelain-
pale cheeks of the Sister-in-Charge of the private
patients' wing at the Princess Beatrice Hospital in
London. 'Sorry,' she said. 'Me putting my big foot in it
again.'

'There'll be another case for Dr Weldon tomorrow if
the other rooms aren't filled. Be sure it's ready, even if
he's an overweight dyspeptic who needs exercise rather
than medication.'

Rebecca turned away, inwardly seething. Paul
Weldon was a good physician, and everyone seemed to
think he was wasting his time with the type of patient
who filled his quota of beds in the private wing. He's my

very good friend, she thought, and I hate to hear what they say behind his back, when girls like Daphne Frost would be all smiles and flirtatious glances when he came in sight.

Rebecca sat down at her desk and opened the report book. She doodled on a pad beside the medical dictionary that she kept handy for the use of nurses and doctors alike, and her eyes were troubled.

What would Paul do with his skills? What did he intend doing with his life, and where did she fit in? She moved restlessly. Daphne was right. There was an air of unrest about the place that Rebecca had never noticed during her years of training at the big old hospital that had taken up her life and dedication for more than four years, first as a nurse in training, when even the disasters had been funny after the event, when she was with other girls doing the same course and getting into the same kind of situations.

She smiled gently. It had been part fun, part agony, but complete fulfilment of her ambition to train and to become a Sister at the dear old hospital, but now all her friends had left or worked in other departments, so that unless they made a date to meet, they seldom saw each other, and most of the carefree medical students with whom they had laughed, danced, eaten cheap food and fallen in and out of love were almost unrecognisable as they made a magic transformation from jeans-clad students to sleek-suited men of importance in their chosen profession.

And now I'm a Sister here. It's what I wanted and what I dreamed of all that time. Rebecca tried to read the report left by the night staff, but the words were meaningless. I'm young, healthy and have the job I wanted. I have good friends, and Paul Weldon, the

best-looking man at Beattie's, says he's in love with me.
She sighed. Maybe it's me who makes the atmosphere
on the wing so edgy now, maybe it's the cold weather,
she thought. She shivered, although the room was
evenly heated and she was hardly ever aware of changes
in temperature. It was chilling to realise that what she
had wasn't enough.

The faint buzz of a bell from one of the rooms made
her shake off her grey thoughts. Another day had begun,
and she must make a round of all the rooms to see that
everything was in order, the right treatments had been
given and the routine of the day was mapped out for all
the staff.

Nurse Frost was coming out of the first room as
Rebecca passed on her way to the well-equipped clinical
room. 'Mr Roper is complaining again that he hasn't had
breakfast, Sister.' The girl raised her eyebrows and
shrugged. 'He's had all that the dietician said he can eat
and he has a fresh jug of pure orange juice on his table,
but he tried to get the ward cleaner to make him some
toast. She told me and I tried to make him see reason,
but he isn't in a very good temper, Sister.'

'I'll see him,' said Rebecca. 'You give out the mail and
flowers and then the morning drug round with the junior
to check.'

'More bloody chrysanths,' muttered Daphne. 'Too
shaggy to arrange, and smell like wet fields.'

'Cheer up! Think of that wonderful date you have and
smile, Nurse.' Rebecca turned away, slightly more
cheerful, and went into the room where Mr Roper lay
like a stranded whale on the narrow white bed with the
almost too pretty floral-print duvet half covering him.

'Good morning, Mr Roper,' said Rebecca, smiling.

'You think it's good, Sister?' He eyed the pretty young

woman with frank appraisal mixed with irritation. No girl had the right to look so fresh, so slim and shapely and yet so businesslike. The coils of bright brown hair that glinted with red lights under the frilled cap hinted at the kind of length that was now too long for fashion, but stunning when loose.

Rebecca returned his gaze and her hazel eyes were amused. 'You've lost five pounds and your blood pressure is going down well,' she said after consulting his notes. 'Now isn't that proof that diet really works?'

'I'll die of weakness if you starve me like this,' he complained. 'I've got a big frame to feed. It's all very well for Dr Weldon to tell me what to do. I bet he eats well and has the odd bottle or two.'

'Dr Weldon jogs and plays squash,' she pointed out gently. 'He also works hard and doesn't sit at a desk all day.'

'That's it, Sister. I sit at a desk and then have to go to business lunches. I can't avoid food,' Mr Roper added self-righteously.

'Well, in here you must stick to a strict diet, and try not to bribe the staff to slip you doughnuts or toast or to bring in bottles of ale.'

'The sneaking little . . . !'

'They have your interests at heart, Mr Roper,' said Rebecca firmly, 'and what's the point of paying for this room if you don't keep to what's ordered?'

She turned as the door opened and Dr Paul Weldon came in. 'Sister Perivale is right,' he said. 'But you aren't really ill, Mr Roper. With will power, you could do all this at home, but without it, may I suggest a few weeks in a health farm under medical supervision?'

Rebecca stared. Paul had the reputation of keeping all his well-heeled paying patients in for as long as possible even if the beds were needed for acute cases. This annoyed the rest of the staff, especially the surgeons, who had a much quicker turn-round of cases and needed more and more beds for really serious conditions.

'Would I have to starve like this, Doctor?' the man asked eagerly.

'You'd have to diet and to exercise and have massage and steam baths and a lot of very pleasant treatments. There'd be other patients with whom you could play bridge or croquet or snooker and make it a holiday.' Paul's smooth voice and bland smile made Rebecca feel suspicious. This wasn't like him, to send a patient away where he would have no further care for him and . . . no further fees.

'You can recommend such a place, Doctor?' asked Mr Roper.

'I have an interest in the Hawthorne Health Spa down in Sussex. They'll take you if you want to go there, and look after you really well.' Paul smiled. 'Think about it, and let Sister know what you decide. You can be under my medical care if that helps, but you'll enjoy your stay there, I'm sure.'

'The *Hawthorne*?' queried Rebecca as soon as they were out of the room. 'It's fantastically expensive and hasn't had a very good reputation.'

'I've bought an interest in the place, and we're stirring things up there.' Paul glanced at the lovely face that now frowned. 'I must talk to you, Becky. Tonight, after duty? I'll pick you up for dinner.'

She opened her mouth to say that she had half prom-ised to call in at the flat of one of the women doctors who lived in a flat overlooking the park, but she had no chance to speak. The figure that came swiftly along the corridor looked like something out of science fiction, as his long white coat belled out behind him, bat-like against the light from the end windows, and the fury of his progress made a nurse carrying a pile of X-rays clutch at them and stand back against the wall, afraid they would be swept up like autumn leaves, in the force of his stormy movements.

'Where's Sister Peregrine?' he demanded.

'I'm Sister Peri*vale*,' said Rebecca, taking a step back to avoid being mown down.

'Well, I want to talk to you about admissions!' He glared at Paul Weldon, who might have been a visitor, a doctor or a patient about to leave, as he seldom wore a white coat on duty. The well-cut suit and smoothly cut hair told of prosperity, well-being and leisure. The glance took in everything, from the silk necktie to the well-polished Gucci shoes, and then turned back to the girl, who stood quite still, wondering who this apparition could be.

'You have an office? Somewhere private?' The voice had lost some of its urgency, and Rebecca was acutely aware of two vivid blue eyes under the thick dark brows.

Paul recovered first and held out a hand. 'I'm Paul Weldon. I have medical beds in this unit,' he said.

'And I believe you've taken some of mine,' said the steely voice. 'I was promised four beds, the ones used by Morton before he was taken ill, and now the girl tells me I have only two.'

'Patients come in needing care and we fill the beds,' said Paul, with a slightly apologetic air. 'I wasn't expecting you to be here so soon.'

'So soon?' The voice was hard again. 'Not soon enough, it would seem. Morton begged me to come as his beds had been under-used for three weeks and he has several cases needing surgery.' He seemed as if he made an effort to be pleasant. 'I'm Anthony Brent, and I shall be here for six weeks while Morton is convalescing. My clinics are at Bart's and my usual private beds are in the new place near Westminster as I've only just returned from overseas.'

'A surgeon,' said Paul, as if that explained the impatience of the man. 'Well, I have just persuaded one patient to leave, so that room will be yours by tomorrow.'

'And the other? I have an anastomosis of gut coming in tomorrow, there's a burst appendix in room one that must go to theatre now and I have at least four hernias waiting for surgery.'

'Room One?' Rebecca called to the nurse who was passing. 'Notes of Room One, and when she was admitted?' she hissed.

The girl looked flustered. 'He brought her in just now, Sister, and wouldn't take no for an answer. I was coming to tell you.'

'When you've finished whispering, can we get down to business?' asked the man with dark hair. 'I have work to do.'

'Nurse tells me you've brought in a patient who's not on our list of admissions for today,' said Rebecca coldly. 'At Beattie's, we don't do it that way. You were lucky to find a room available.' Paul went back into the room where Mr Roper was deciding that a health spa was what he needed, and Rebecca closed her office door as soon as she was there with this strange force that had come to the wing.

The report book was where she had left it and, to her horror, she saw an envelope that she hadn't noticed.

I must have seen it if it was there before I left the office, she told herself. As her hand went out to it, another hand got there first, and touched the edge of the envelope, flicking it over to see the address, and as Rebecca tried to pick it up, a tug made her drop it.

'I thought you said you didn't know about my admission?' asked the cool voice. 'Perhaps the Sisters at Beattie's don't read reports or go over their morning mail before seeing patients and being ready for doctors' rounds? I see I shall have to learn what you do here, Sister.'

The envelope was flipped over to her, and she opened it to find the usual flimsy admission form inside announcing that Sister Faith from the Convent of St Mary-the-Martyr was to be expected that morning.

'And to save time, I brought her in myself,' said Mr Brent. 'Do I have to admit her, prepare her for theatre and do the operation?'

The tap on the door was followed by Nurse Frost peeping in. 'I'm sorry, Sister,' she said. 'The note on your desk got caught up in the mail for Mr Tyler and I brought it along as soon as he told me.' Her face cleared. 'Oh, you've seen it. Do you want me to prepare her for the theatre? Sister rang down and said the operation is scheduled for eleven this morning.'

'Yes, please,' said Rebecca. 'Usual precautions, and ask if she's eaten anything this morning. I'll be along as soon as I can.'

'So you didn't know.' The tone was flat and uncompromising. 'I suppose I owe you an apology.'

'It really isn't necessary. Time is short if she's to be in theatre relaxed and dressed,' said Rebecca. She had the oddest feeling that if he apologised, the barrier that had formed between them the moment he had called her Sister Peregrine and looked at her with such arrogance might crumble, and barriers were safe . . . dividing and protecting, as well as isolating in a kind of loneliness.

Rebecca pushed back her chair and made for the door. 'I'll come with you,' said Mr Brent. 'Another strange face might be too much for the poor lady.'

Wordlessly, Rebecca followed him to the room where now a flurry of organised care was in progress. So he thinks my face would frighten her and I'm too dim to walk along the corridor on my own! she thought.

Sister Faith was lying in bed, pale and listless with two bright spots of hectic colour in her thin cheeks, making the pallor even more evident. She held up a hand that seemed all skin and blue veins and it fell on to the bedcover again without strength. The notes, which Rebecca had read hastily, showed a picture of a woman who had been in pain for several months with a niggling discomfort occasionally erupting into agony, all of which she had tried to ignore until she collapsed and had to tell her Mother Superior that she couldn't go on with her work.

'Suspected acute appendix with possible peritonitis', the notes stated, and the rise in temperature and pulse rate and the general condition of the woman on the bed showed clearly that an acute inflammation of the pelvis was certain. Why go on so long? Rebecca wondered. Surely Sister Faith must have known that she had appendicitis? The face on the pillow under the linen cap was intelligent and gentle, and Rebecca noticed with a sense of amazement that the manner of the man who now stood by the door had changed. He kept a distance as if afraid of offending the patient's modesty, and his face showed no sign of his former irritation.

He looked at the covered trolley that held the sterile equipment for preparation for operation and then at the nurse who stood, masked and gloved, ready to paint the abdominal skin with antiseptic skin paint. Rebecca half smiled. It might be acceptable for a man to watch the routine when the patient was a man or woman admitted in the usual way, but this lady was a nun and must, because of her vocation, be unwilling for a man to look at her half-naked body.

'I'll be in your office, Sister,' said Anthony Brent, backing away and suddenly selfconscious. Rebecca nodded and waited until the door was closed after him before telling the nurse to get on with the preparation.

'You've been in a lot of pain?' asked Rebecca gently.

'Nothing I couldn't bear,' said the weak voice. 'I couldn't come home as we were overwhelmed by the sick and dying, and it was one of the doctors who sent a report about my health to the Mother Superior back home, and she sent for me immediately.'

'And you collapsed a few days ago and have had infusions of glucose, saline and mineral salts before coming in here.' Rebecca looked puzzled. 'Where were you when you were so ill?'

The figure on the bed winced as the cold swab saturated with acriflavine washed gently over her lower abdomen. 'I was in the Sudan with others of my Order, working with refugees,' Sister Faith said at last. 'My suffering is nothing compared with what we saw and tried to help each day.' Her eyes filled with weak tears. 'I failed to keep healthy, Sister. Who can serve if they're ill themselves? It was God's will for me to go there, and now I have to bow to this.'

Rebecca removed the small sterile towel from the kidney dish holding the disposable syringe. She swabbed the thin arm with spirit and skilfully injected the premedication drug of omnopon and scopolamine. As she withdrew the needle, she glanced at the serene face and wondered how any woman could suffer so much and yet be calm and philosophical.

Nurse Frost covered the purified skin with a sterile towel and binder and slipped a clean white theatre gown over the painfully thin body. 'You will leave my cap on, Sister? I'm not allowed to appear before others with an uncovered head,' said Sister Faith.

'Nurse will leave it on and put a theatre turban over it,' promised Rebecca. She smiled and held the hand on the coverlet. 'Another hour and you'll be in theatre, and after it, you can look forward to recovery.'

'You're so good,' said Sister Faith. 'A born nurse, and the kind we so badly need out there.'

'Not for me,' said Rebecca, and wondered why she felt sad. 'I wouldn't do. I speak only English and a little French and German, and I could never cope with people from a different culture.' She recalled television programmes about the terrible drought and disease in Ethiopia and the Sudan, and knew she could never have the courage to go there to work.

'I shall pray that you help us,' said the drowsy voice, as the premedication began to dull the senses and take the edge off reality.

'Rather a nice old duck,' said Nurse Frost as she cleared the trolley. 'I hope she does well.'

Rebecca laughed. 'How irreverent!—but I know what you mean. She's sweet, and so completely self-sacrificing it makes me feel humble.'

'Not me,' asserted Nurse Frost. 'Charity begins at home. You won't find me in a mud hut with all those mosquitoes buzzing around my head!' She looked defiant as if she was resisting the urge to be charitable. 'One thing, though, Sister. She has no flowers in her room and none delivered. You'd think the nuns would send her something, wouldn't you?'

'I believe nuns take a vow of poverty and chastity, Nurse Frost, so they would think it an unnecessary luxury.'

'We could give her all those fresh ones that came for Mr Roper,' Nurse Frost went on in the same offhand tone. 'He's going to some poncy spa and won't miss them.'

'Ask him first,' warned Rebecca. 'It's often the richest patients who walk out with every last limp flower and the remains of their sweets, but I'm sure he'll be glad to let her have them.' She smiled. 'He wants to be liked. Some men are like big huggy-bears who growl but really want to be loved. Mr Roper eats too much to make up for other things lacking, I suspect.'

'Well, don't forget one big bear in your office, Sister. I wouldn't try hugging him if I were you. He's mean, that one, but gorgeous,' added Nurse Frost cheerfully, and tapped on Mr Roper's door.

Rebecca brushed down the front of her well-fitting white dress and twitched the closely-buckled belt in place. It was as bad as going for an interview, she decided—seams straight in her very sheer tights, shoes clean and well polished and her hair sleek and well-behaved.

She took a deep breath and opened the door. Mr Anthony Brent sat at her desk, in her revolving chair, with her telephone to his ear, his feet on *her* desk, and was obviously in the middle of enjoying *her* coffee. He looked up and nodded curtly. 'Get another cup. I need to talk to you,' he said, and went on with his telephone conversation.

At any other time Rebecca would have gone to the

ward kitchen for the cup, but this man seemed to have taken over and thought of her as a kind of idiot servant, so she pressed the bell that brought the junior running to the office, and asked her for fresh coffee and biscuits for one.

There was only one other chair and Rebecca had to sit straight on a pre-formed plastic seat that was slippery and obviously designed to discourage anyone from sitting there for too long and wasting time.

Mr Brent put down the phone. 'Nice quiet office,' he remarked. 'I can do most of my phoning from here, as I have to check with Bart's when I'm on call.'

'There's a telephone in reception for staff outside use,' said Rebecca coldly. 'This one is strictly for the use of the wing here, and unless there's an emergency, it's reserved for incoming calls.'

'We have an emergency, or don't you consider that Sister Faith is very ill? I had to let her Mother Superior know what was happening.' His eyes took in every detail of her dress, her figure and her hair, and Rebecca found that she couldn't meet his gaze. It was so silly—he was rude and inconsiderate, and yet she felt drawn to him, as if . . . as if this meeting was long overdue and would lead to others. The tray of coffee arrived, and she found it useful as a means to control her hands and appear normal. I don't panic over men with deep blue eyes, I never have minded being insulted when I know it's in the heat of the moment, I can make most men smile at me and be charming, so why does my heart do strange things when he brushes his hair back with a suntanned hand and watches me so closely? she wondered.

'Sister Faith is half asleep and prepared for theatre,' she said. 'Theatre Sister will ring down when they're ready for her.'

'Then I'll wait here until she rings us, as that will give me time to scrub. What's the staff like up there?'

'Very efficient, Mr Brent. I think you'll find we're good at our work at the Princess Beatrice.'

He laughed. 'Of course! Everywhere's the same. We have blinding loyalty to our own training schools, even if they don't come up to the mark sometimes.'

'Beattie's is the best hospital you could find anywhere,' said Rebecca, trying not to be annoyed, but she knew her colour was rising and she longed to throw something at the arrogant face.

'So I hear,' he said, 'but I'm just a stranger here and need to be shown how good it all is. I need to be made welcome, given good strong coffee when I feel weak and have staff jumping when I say jump.'

'You seem to have managed on your own very well, Mr Brent,' said Rebecca, looking pointedly at the empty coffee pot and the plate that had once held biscuits.

Mr Brent reached over and took three of her biscuits. 'I need them to take me through this op,' he said solemnly. 'Good of you to think of sending for more.'

'If you've finished using my office, may I have it back?' she asked, but her smile was fixed and she was aware of a kind of panic threatening to show in her face. He was taking over as if this was his right. Other surgeons came and sat in the office, had coffee with her and used the telephone, so what made this man any different?

Slowly he stretched and stood tall, and against the light from the window he seemed even bigger than when he had come down the corridor. The plastic chair was hard against her back as Rebecca tried to merge with it away from his touch as he came to her and rested a hand on her shoulder, then touched the smooth swathe of hair at the back of her crisp Sister's cap.

'My sisters all have short hair,' he said. 'Are you really just an old-fashioned girl?' He laughed and left her blushing and angry, but she couldn't decide if the anger was because he touched her as if he knew her well, or because she wished he knew her better, and she hated her own reaction.

So I'm an idiot, I'm old-fashioned and bad-mannered because I didn't fall over him and let him take over the entire wing, she thought. Maybe he doesn't like women and treats them all like this. She glanced up at the wall clock and knew she had many people to see, work to be done, and half an hour later she had read her mail, made notes about the new admissions and was ready when the telephone rang to go with Sister Faith up to the operating theatre.

'She's almost asleep,' whispered Nurse Frost.

'I'll go with the trolley, Nurse,' said Rebecca. Daphne Frost raised her eyebrows. Usually the Sister of the private wing left that to the other nurses. 'She must feel strange and a little apprehensive,' said Rebecca, to give herself an excuse to go with the nun, but one glance at the softly relaxed face under the linen cap and disposable theatre turban showed that Sister Faith was almost happy and lived up to her name. She had complete faith in the staff, the surgeon and her own beliefs and was ready for anything.

'I'll get Mr Roper packed up, Sister. He's going after lunch, and Mr Brent has a case coming in soon after.'

Rebecca raised her shoulders in a helpless shrug. Mr Brent really did make his presence felt, and Nurse Frost seemed to enjoy it.

'Very well, Nurse, and I'll be back to do Mrs Mac-Donald's dressing. She might be fit to go out in a few days if the fistula has healed.'

If Mrs MacDonald leaves, there'll be a bed for one of the cases that Mr Brent mentioned, she thought. Mrs MacDonald was the last case that Mr Morton had done before he went off sick and she had to stay until her wound had healed completely. Why am I mentally wishing her out of her room? thought Rebecca. One of the nicest of the patients and a joy to see getting fit again.

The wing doesn't revolve round one man, she told herself firmly. She helped the porter with the trolley into the anaesthetic room and placed a hand on Sister Faith's, squeezing it gently. An answering squeeze, faint but positive, and a slight smile was the reply, but the tired eyes remained closed.

Rebecca stepped back softly, leaving the nurse to attend to the needs of the anaesthetist, who was ready with face mask and gas machines.

He shook his head when the nurse held up a syringe of thiopentone. The patient was so relaxed and now asleep that the gentle gases would be enough for the first induction.

At the door, Rebecca looked towards the circle of bright light coming through the porthole window to the theatre and saw figures moving, dressed in theatre green. One figure, taller than the rest, stood with tightly gloved hands in front of him, calm and confident. For a moment she thought he looked at her, but she knew that from the theatre he would see only the round window, and it was steaming up rapidly.

She went out into the darker corridor. He would be gone in six weeks. He would walk out of her life as easily as he had burst into it. She walked back to the wing and went through her duties efficiently, smiling and saying all the right things, but her mind was busy with such peculiar thoughts that she wondered if she was going mad.

His sisters had short hair. She giggled. Did he mean his own sisters or the Sisters in the various units where he worked? Did he appear with a pair of long shears in the clinical room of a ward and firmly clip off any locks that hung below a Sister's cap?

She touched the smooth hair tightly pinned into a gleaming coil that added to her dignity and was tidy at all times on duty. Mr Brent had touched it as if he couldn't keep his fingers away. Was it because he thought it would be better short . . . or did he secretly love a woman to have long hair?

CHAPTER TWO

'THEY'VE been in theatre for a long time, Sister. I saw one of the theatre nurses at lunch and she said they hadn't closed up yet. Poor little woman, she looked so frail on the trolley, and she must be in a mess inside.' Nurse Frost handed over some new X-rays and asked the Sister of the private patients' wing for the keys to the drug cupboard. 'I'll give out the lunchtime medicines before you go to lunch, and be ready to receive Sister Faith back into her room.'

'Good idea,' said Rebecca. 'I'll check the DDA drugs and go down to the dining room as soon as you have them all on the tray. Take the new junior with you and make her check them again, but as you say, it's a good idea to be clear before Sister Faith comes back, unless they send her to Intensive Care.'

'Nurse Brown said there was no panic. Just a mass of adhesions that had formed ever the past year or so, and they've given her some blood.'

'Is she in good hands, do you think?' asked Rebecca, trying to sound mildly interested.

'Brown has fallen like a ton of bricks! We're due to meet some people tonight, and she'll bore us to death drooling over him. It's always the same with her,' Daphne Frost added, laughing. 'A new face that's masculine, a deep brown voice that speaks to her, if only to ask for a swab, and she's a pushover!'

'Nurse Brown is very pretty,' said Rebecca, and wondered why she wished theatre nurses with big blue eyes

22

couldn't spend so much time watching surgeons over the green masks that enhanced the eyes and hid any bad features.

'He's cool, very cool,' said Daphne Frost. 'Cool enough to burn.' She giggled. 'I'm glad I have a boy-friend and am getting married next year, or I could join the flock!'

Rebecca checked the drugs and made sure her dress was immaculate and her shoes showed no signs of dirt before she walked slowly down the corridor and to the lift. Everywhere was quiet and the soft pastels and pretty curtains by the big corridor windows gave an air of peace and welcome. The small passenger elevator stood with the door open and from below she heard the rattle of the door as someone tried to signal to her to close it and allow it to go down.

She stepped inside and pressed the button for the floor she needed, thinking how different all the equipment was in the PP wing from the solid but ancient mahogany splendour of the original part of the hospital. The lift sighed gently and the door was opened.

'Oh, it's you, Becky. I've rattled this door for ages, but some goon left it open and I thought I'd have to walk.'

Paul looked very annoyed. 'It's all yours,' said Rebecca lightly. 'Take it before someone rattles from above and calls you a goon!'

'Becky? Come back! You haven't said what time we'll meet tonight.'

'I haven't said I'm free,' she replied.

'Rubbish! Of course you're free. Make it nine o'clock, will you? I have to see someone first. Meet you by the main entrance, not the hostel.' He slammed the door shut and pressed the button he needed, leaving Rebecca standing there watching his tall figure disappear as if he was being beamed up to outer space.

She went to the self-service restaurant used by all the staff and picked up soup and rolls and cheese. 'Not hungry?' asked the Sister of Men's Surgical.

'Not very,' admitted Rebecca.

'What's wrong? You look a bit ruffled . . . if that's the right word for someone who never has a hair out of place!'

'We're busy, Maeve, and we have a new surgeon who's making himself felt more than somewhat.'

Maeve O'Riley laughed. 'Six feet two of butch charm? Don't tell me you've not fallen for those deep blue eyes?'

'If you mean Mr Brent, the answer is no,' said Rebecca shortly.

'Ah, he's a lovely man, a lovely man,' said Maeve comfortably. 'He'd do anything for anyone, that man. We all adore him.'

'I haven't caught that particular disease,' said Rebecca.

'Of course not. You have Paul, so what would you want with him? Paul's quite as good-looking, in his own way, of course. Different, but what two men are the same?' Maeve rattled on and finished her fish and chips before Rebecca had drunk all her soup. 'Mind you, I wonder if our Dr Weldon will be here for much longer. There are rumours. Come on, Ducky, tell me what's in the wind. You of all people would know if he's leaving.'

Maeve eyed her, her face bright with curiosity.

'I don't know, Maeve.' Rebecca saw the girl's disbelief. 'It's true! I'm the last to know anything here. I wish people wouldn't take it for granted that there's anything between Paul and me. We're good friends who go out together sometimes,' she said, and knew she sounded weak.

'He takes it for granted,' said Maeve. She gave her friend a shrewd look. 'You can't be seen in public with a man like that and not have the whole place knowing what goes on between you, or inventing it if they don't find out enough.' She sighed. 'I like Paul and he's a very good doctor, but you should make him leave all those hypochondriacs to their shrinks and loving wives. It's no work for a really good doctor.'

'I have no influence with him and I don't want any,' said Rebecca vehemently. 'We're friends and no more.'

'Not from where I'm sitting,' said Maeve. She pushed her plate aside. 'Coffee? I'll bring two.'

A week ago I wouldn't have reacted like that, thought Rebecca. A week or even a day or so ago, I would have been flattered that they thought I was Paul's choice and done nothing to deny it, but now I don't even want to meet him tonight. She crumbled the rest of her bread roll and ate a piece she didn't need. Was it the sight of Paul in the lift, urbane and sure of himself, but putting on the merest ounce or two that showed, and the fact that he was too lazy to walk up two short flights of stairs if the lift was unobtainable? Or was it that he took her so much for granted these days, as if he owned her?

'You like it very strong and black,' said Maeve. 'I don't know how you drink it.' She stirred a double helping of cream into her own cup and added sugar. 'I shouldn't, but I must,' she said cheerfully. 'Mr Brent has his black. That you have in common!'

'And that's all,' said Rebecca.

'He'll be leaving too, almost before he's said hello,' grumbled Maeve. 'We could do with him here all the time—he's much more photogenic than Mr Morton.'

'Don't tell me you carry his picture close to your heart?' Rebecca smiled. 'Been sneaking up behind him to take his picture? My, you are smitten!'

'Don't be silly. It's just that he hasn't the time to get to the chemist today. Early closing, you remember? So my nurse collected his snaps for him when she was off duty.' Maeve giggled. 'One look at these and there'll be badly cracked hearts littering up the whole of Beattie's, bless her old heart.'

'Holiday snaps?' asked Rebecca.

'I'm not so sure.' Maeve frowned. 'Take a peep. He'll never know unless you tell him, and why shouldn't we have a look?'

'I don't think——' began Rebecca.

'Go on, you know you're dying to look!' Maeve glanced towards the door as if afraid Anthony Brent would appear, then handed over the folder of prints.

Rebecca saw a vast expanse of sand with a huge tent in the foreground and a table and chairs. Anthony Brent sat by the table dressed in shorts and a bush shirt, and by his side was a pretty girl in a simple white dress. It was impossible to see the dress well as she sat on the other side of the table, but it was as plain as a uniform and not really holiday gear.

'Did he say where?' asked Rebecca. Maeve shook her head.

'Somewhere in the Middle East, I suppose. Egypt or the Gulf, and there's one with several men in long white djellabas. Maybe he took her up the Nile. Lucky girl!'

'Just three?' asked Rebecca.

'That's all, but they all have the girl in them. He said they were reprints that he wants to send off quickly to someone, and I guess it isn't being sent to that camel!'

Rebecca handed them back. 'I must go. We have a

theatre case coming back soon and I want to be there.'

'Is that Sister Faith?'

'Do you know her?' asked Rebecca.

'I met her before her last trip to the Sudan and I must come up to see her when she's fit for visitors. Will you give her my love, Becky?'

'Certainly. She'll be glad of a familiar face later. I wonder why she isn't in the general ward? Surely nuns who take a vow of poverty can't afford private rooms?'

'It isn't that,' said Maeve. 'They can't be put in with anyone outside the convent, and Beattie's has a fund for such cases, endowed by members of her church, so that nuns can have privacy and individual care even if they half-starve themselves for the rest of their lives. She would willingly go into a general ward, but she might be embarrassed, especially when male visitors come and she's in bed. Not nice for those who choose the cloister.'

'It's a fund that really is of use,' agreed Rebecca. 'She's so patient, so sweet that I should hate to think of her being humiliated.'

The lift door was open and Rebecca went up to her own floor. A man dashed past the lift door as she opened it and she saw a tall figure in green theatre clothes running along to her wing. She half smiled. Anthony Brent hadn't wasted time fuming at the closed lift doors, he had run down the stairs from the theatre block and along the corridor as swift and effortlessly as a panther. She laughed softly. Not a pink panther . . . just a theatre green one, in rubber boots.

She quickened her steps. If Mr Brent was running to her ward, then it meant that Sister Faith was out of the theatre and might need her. She heard the main elevator humming and the doors swish back and knew that the

theatre trolley was on its way down again from the
theatre with the patient.

The room was neat and ready, with the door back
against the wall and the bed pushed to one side to make
entry easy. The soft duvet was being folded back and the
electric blanket taken away. Rebecca noted the drip
stand and the tray of drugs and disposable syringes that
might be needed for post-operative care and the fact that
the water jug was as far as possible from the bed so that
no water could be given until the immediate possibility
of nausea after anaesthetic was over.

Unconscious, Sister Faith looked even smaller, and
the theatre porter lifted her with the help of Nurse Frost
as if she weighed no more than a bag of feathers. The
drip into her arm flowed well and was secure, and the
man in the green theatre tunic and trousers stepped
back, satisfied.

'Good,' said Mr Brent. 'Well done, Nurse.' He smiled
at Nurse Frost, then saw Rebecca watching from the
doorway. He raised his eyebrows in mock surprise.
'Everything fine and ready,' he observed.

'You obviously didn't expect it to be,' said Rebecca.
'If you'll write up her notes, we'll try to carry out the
correct post-operative treatment too,' she added coldly.
'Actually, we're quite efficient.'

She looked at the chart and bent to feel the pulse of
the woman on the bed, then took her pen from the top
pocket of her uniform dress and recorded the first dot on
the chart, with the time, the rate of respirations and the
rate of flow of the transfusion.

'Thank you, Sister.' Anthony Brent took the pen from
her hand and turned away. 'See you in the office to brief
you,' he said.

'That's a good pen. I'd make sure you get it back,

Sister. *Men*! They pinch anything, from pens to bums.'
Nurse Frost laughed. 'Sorry, Sister. He isn't that sort.
They said he did a marvellous job and Sister Faith should
be everlastingly grateful.'

'Hush! Not in front of someone coming round from
anaesthetic, Nurse,' whispered Rebecca. 'Remember,
they hear more than we realise. I'll leave you to special
her for an hour or so until the agency special arrives. A
quarter-hourly pulse and respiration, four-hourly
temperature—and watch that drip.'

The office door was shut and through the frosted glass
Rebecca could make out a blur of green. She hesitated,
suddenly reluctant to go into her own domain, but it was
ridiculous to have to tap on her own door and wait for
someone to say, 'Come in.' She pushed open the door
and saw that once again Mr Brent had taken over. Even
one drawer was open and a pile of its contents sat
precariously on the only other chair.

'You might get some bigger sheets of paper, Sister.
This notepaper isn't really adequate for my needs. I have
to write to the Convent and to a colleague who knows
Sister Faith.'

'If you wouldn't mind putting back my personal belongings, including my own notepaper, Mr Brent, and
look in the rack at the back of the desk, you'll see the full
range of hospital forms and notepaper!'

'I'll leave that to you. I've made a mess, I'm afraid,
and you know the order you want everything. Here are
her notes, and I'd like these two letters included in the
post.'

He swung from her chair and was close to her. 'My
pen?' she asked, with icy sweetness.

'Yours?' He examined it carefully. 'It could be, but it's
a good one. So many leave smudges and slip in the

fingers. This is the first silver one that doesn't.'

'I find it useful,' said Rebecca.

'Pity. I was growing quite fond of it.' He grinned and pushed the pen back into her breast pocket, slowly and carefully, his hand lingering to make sure the pen was firmly in place, and Rebecca felt the soft pressure on the fullness under the close-fitting uniform. She knew her colour was rising and tried not to breathe deeply. Anthony Brent stepped away. 'The notes are explicit and should give no cause for concern. We had to leave a drainage tube in situ as there's an abscess in the Pouch of Douglas, but the adhesions have all been broken down and the appendix removed, with difficulty.'

'Post-operative pain?' she asked.

'I've written her up for two dosages. She's small and may need very little for her body weight, but the op did involve quite a lot of handling, although I was as gentle as possible, so use your discretion, Sister, and give the higher dose if you think she needs it.' He became aware of his theatre boots. 'Sorry about this. I know Sisters who'd have my guts for garters if I wore them on the ward! My own sisters would carve me up too and tell me I'm an inconsiderate slob,' he added cheerfully.

'I like the sound of your Sisters,' said Rebecca. She began to put things away in her drawer and knew he was still in the office, watching her. She wished it wasn't the deep bottom drawer to the desk that he had cleared, as she had to bend down to it or sit on her heels, neither attitude being very dignified and both revealing the tightness of her skirt and the shape of her hips and legs.

She heard the door open and shut, and breathed deeply. An old diary and a packet of letters from nurses with whom she had trained were placed with the other items, and she closed the drawer. A few more minutes and she had tidied the desk top and read the new notes. The office was hers again, neat and efficient, almost clinical. She smoothed back her sleek hair and sat at the desk. Was she too clinical, she wondered, and did it matter that a man came and cluttered up her desk and touched her with gentle hands?

She took the pen from her top pocket and rolled it between her fingers, then, making sure the cap was secure, she put it in the pocket of her skirt as if afraid that someone might take it from its rightful place and touch her, making her want to take the hand and beg him not to go. This is stupid, she thought angrily. He annoys me, and yet I can feel his sexuality. That's it! Any woman would be aware of him in that way, and it isn't necessary to like a man to feel that. Nothing alters my first impression of him, and men like him think they can get away with a lot just because they ooze masculinity in a setting where women are in the majority.

Rebecca went to check the patients and sat with Sister Faith for a while to relieve Nurse Frost for a tea break. The nun lay inert, but her eyes were now open and her expression showed pain even when she refused to admit it.

Rebecca checked the weaker of the drugs with one of the nurses and injected it into the intravenous tube. The sunken eyes widened and then closed and the breathing became regular and deeper as Sister Faith relaxed and slept.

'What was she doing in the Sudan?' asked Nurse Frost when she came back from tea.

'She belongs to an Order who send nuns out to hospitals run on next to no funds to help under-developed countries, or to areas where famine causes health problems.' Rebecca sighed. 'She looks like a famine victim herself! I'm going to my room for a couple of hours so that I can relieve you this evening, Nurse Frost. I may need an extra hour next week when I meet some friends up from Devon, so you needn't think I'm being self-sacrificing.'

'No hurry, Sister. I can write a letter while I sit here, and I haven't a date tonight.' Nurse Frost looked up from the notes. 'You have a date, Sister, but mine is off.'

'Not until after duty, and I can leave everything ready when I go over now.'

Does the whole hospital know that Paul's picking me up this evening? she wondered resentfully, and put up her umbrella as the rain started again, making the path to the hostel behind the path labs puddled and slippery. That was another thing. Paul had asked her to meet him at the main entrance to the hospital, where he could bring his car round, and he wouldn't have to walk this path with her to and from the hostel. He might get rain spots on his nice new shoes, she thought, and decided that all men were poison.

Rebecca looked in her wardrobe and wondered where Paul would be taking her to dinner. Sometimes he liked to go to a carvery in one of the big hotels like the Cumberland, but when he wanted to impress other people he included in his invitations, he favoured smaller, more exclusive places that served Nouvelle Cuisine, and dishes with exotic names that usually turned out to be a small helping of a mixture of attractive-looking food, reminding Rebecca more of a flower arrangement than a good meal.

She smiled. Paul enjoyed good food and she suspected he preferred the hearty roasts of a carvery but was eager to impress with his knowledge of food and wine at the other restaurants and clubs. In time, she decided, Paul would be a very solid citizen indeed if he didn't watch his waistline!

The skirt of soft suede, warm and elegant in muted green, and the mohair sweater of rust would do nicely for the carvery, but he had hinted that he wanted her to meet someone, so this time he would expect a dress to catch the eye. Rebecca fingered her latest buy, a fitting gown of deep purple crêpe that hugged her hips and tied like a sarong over her thighs. The bodice was plain but sat snugly over her curving breasts and accentuated the small waist. With it she could wear heavy gilt junk jewellery or a more restrained necklace of real turquoise and silver, that matched a Victorian pin of the same stones, shaped like a butterfly. The pin could be used as a brooch or the back unscrewed to house a hairclip that secured it either to her coil of hair or, if she felt bold, to a thick tress of her long hair.

I'll wear the dress and the turquoise, she decided, guessing that this evening was important to Paul even if it wouldn't be for her.

She made tea and sipped it slowly, then showered so that she could dress quickly for her date and be ready even if she was late off duty. It was time for duty, so once more the umbrella went up and she braved the rain, hoping her tights were not splashed and carrying her duty shoes of white kid in a bag and wearing heavy walking shoes.

A car sped away from the main door with a discharged patient, her husband and two beaming children. Rebecca smiled as she waved, sensing their warmth and joy at being reunited. Families were good. If she married Paul, she could have children and everything she needed to make life easy, so why had she kept him at arm's length for so long?

The office in the wing was empty and lights in the corridors showed pink and cosy as the evening drew curtains and excluded the rain. Sister Faith was awake and sipping mineral water from a beaker held by Nurse Frost. 'The special didn't come, Sister, but sent a message that she has a sore throat, but we managed. The case we expected had to go to his nearest hospital in Kent as he was in crisis, and Mr Brent's other cases don't come in until tomorrow.'

'I'm afraid I'm taking all your attention,' said Sister Faith in a weak voice.

'You're less trouble than the whole of the wing,' said Nurse Frost firmly. 'It's nice to have someone who really does as she's told and drinks up her nice mineral water even though she hates it.' She held the beaker to the dry mouth again. 'A little more, if you can, but don't force it,' she said tenderly.

'I'll take over, Nurse,' said Rebecca. 'Go off duty, and thank you for your help.'

'Are you sure, Sister? Well, if you are, I'll just catch the paper shop open, and later I shall try the new takeaway down the hill.'

'Such a kind girl,' said Sister Faith. 'If she had a vocation, we could make use of her.'

'In England or abroad?' asked Rebecca.

'Both, but we need young healthy women who can stand the heat and dust of the Sudan, Ethiopia or any of the places where we have Missions. Not that they have to be of our religion or from a convent at all.' The nun looked at Rebecca and smiled. 'You'd do very well, Sister.'

'Not me! I have too much in London, and I have no knowledge of tropical diseases,' said Rebecca, shaking her head.

'A lot of nurses help Voluntary Service Overseas,' hinted Sister Faith.

'Some of my friends went, but they have to go for two years, which is far too long to give up in a career,' replied Rebecca. 'If they land up in some terrible place, it may be bearable for one year, but at the end of that period it must be agony to know you have to go through all that again for another year.' She blushed. 'I'm sorry. You have to go where you're sent for as long as you're needed, Sister, but that's where we differ. Six months would be my limit, and even then I'd need to have the option of leaving if it wasn't for me.'

'Six months could save a lot of lives,' said Sister Faith simply.

'Sleep now,' said Rebecca. She checked the drip and noticed that the woman's skin was less dry and wrinkled after her body had absorbed the fluids. Her pulse rate was still rapid and showed that the inflammation would take time to clear, but the drain was producing a steady amount of discharge into the bottle of disinfectant under the bed, and she was drinking fluids freely now with no nausea.

The notes showed that Dr Boris Pilatczech had given the anaesthetic, and that accounted for the swift return to full consciousness and the lack of sickness after operation. Dear Doctor Boris, thought Rebecca affectionately. He was the most popular doctor at Beattie's and one of the dishiest, even now that he had a family and his dark hair was silvery at the temples. At least dear Mr Brent couldn't find a thing wrong with the theatre staff!

Rebecca closed the report book and saw that Nurse Frost had left the photos for Mr Brent on the desk. There was no way of telling if he knew they were there waiting for him, and Maeve had said he wanted them in a hurry. He wants everything in a hurry, thought Rebecca. If he was in love, he would sweep a woman off balance and carry her off before she knew what had happened. She let out a shuddering breath. He wouldn't wait patiently for weeks and months as Paul did, until the moment was right and the time suited him to ask a girl to marry him.

She picked up the phone and asked Reception to bleep Mr Brent for the private wing, then did her evening round, before supper went in for the patients.

The room where Mr Roper had been was empty and ready for the admission of a hernia case the next day. The next room was empty too, as Mrs Baxter had been transferred to a convalescent home in Bournemouth to recover from her hip replacement and so another room would be available for Mr Brent. Rebecca wondered if the arrangements for Mrs Baxter had been made quickly because he had the girl in Reception under his spell too.

'Good evening, Mr Syms,' she said brightly as she closed the room door and advanced towards the bed where a very jaundiced man was sitting up, reading. Rebecca didn't touch the bed or the patient, but she saw that there were fresh gowns and masks on the table by the window ready for nurses to wear when they made the bed or gave blanket baths. Jugs of iced water, fresh fruit juices and mineral water were within his reach and a bowl of grapes and oranges was temptingly arranged by his side.

'This is the fifth day of jaundice, I believe,' she said.

'I look ghastly, but in fact I feel better,' said the patient. 'I was a bit miserable before the jaundice appeared, but now it's as if it released something and I don't feel so bad.' He picked a grape from the bowl.

'How long must I stay in purdah, Sister? If I had leprosy, I wouldn't be so restricted!'

'If you were at home, you could move about more so long as you took the usual precautions about washing well after going to the lavatory and not using the same crockery as others in the same house, but here, with so many patients, we can't take chances, and you must remain in this room until the jaundice is gone and the stool samples are free of the bug. Then, give or take six or seven days, you can go back to work and mingle with others, but you should give your liver a chance to calm down, and all alcohol must be avoided for six months or a year, or whatever time the doctor tells you is sufficient.'

'Groans all round!' sighed Mr Syms. 'I do enjoy a glass of champers and a nightcap of whisky—and what about food?'

'Keep off red meat and fats and cream and eat plenty of vegetables and carbohydrates,' Rebecca told him.

'I can't live on a bowl of rice and a few sticks of celery!' He looked really annoyed. 'I enjoy my food and I eat what I know is good for me. Why should I get this when I've never really eaten or drunk too much, but always the best quality, Sister?'

'You went abroad for a holiday and ate something infected. It can happen to anyone.' Rebecca regarded him with sympathy. 'It was unfortunate, but it will be in your own interests to do as the doctor tells you. Dr Weldon does know about infectious hepatitis and is very good, you know.' She saw he was restless. 'Have you everything you need? I brought in a new copy of the *Radio Times* and Nurse can put on any of the videos you choose.' She gave him a brilliant smile. 'I can't promise any other entertainment, but there are some good programmes tonight.'

'I'd rather you stayed and talked to me. Could you
pop in after duty?'

Rebecca shook her head. 'Sorry, Mr Syms, I have to
go out.'

'A date? Lucky devil. I suppose sex is also forbidden
while this lasts?'

'Unless your lady has the same condition,' she said,
and laughed. She heard the heated food trolley in the
corridor and managed to get away from the almost
physical bond that Mr Syms tried to make in his need for
company. She supervised the diets, and couldn't help
smiling when she saw that Mr Syms had boiled rice with
tomato puree and braised celery hearts for supper. It
looked delicious, but she knew he wanted something
with meat in it.

The other food was really appetising, and everyone
who was allowed full diet had chicken Kiev and stuffed
aubergines and a variety of salads.

'Has Mr Brent bleeped?' she asked the nurse giving
out suppers.

'No, Sister. He hasn't been in since looking at Sister
Faith's drainage tube half an hour ago.'

'Oh, dear, I asked Reception to say he was wanted
here.'

'He was in a hurry and might not have come in through
the main corridor. It's shorter by the side door and up
the stairs.' The nurse smiled. 'He runs everywhere,
unlike our nice Dr Weldon who takes life much more
calmly, and gets what he wants without fuss.'

So some adore Paul and some fall at the feet of our
new tempestuous surgeon, thought Rebecca. She took
the photos and rang through to Reception again. 'Where
does Mr Brent have a room? Someone left a package for
him here and I think he wants it,' she said.

'He has a room in the hostel, but he has a flat nearer his own hospital, Bart's. Now let me see. Room Twenty-four.'

Rebecca gasped. 'In my corridor?' she said.

'That's right. He's using Mr Morton's room while he's away sick. I can't spare anyone to go over now, Sister. Could you drop it in on your way off duty?'

'I suppose so. Yes, of course I can,' she added hastily, as her first words were ungracious. She walked away from the office, having left the folder on her desk. Don't be silly, she told herself. Anyone would think you're scared of him. He can't *do* anything, or give you hepatitis or some horrid lurgy—but when she was ready to go off duty, the Night Sister called her into Sister Faith's room to help her with the bed before they settled her for the night.

'I knew you wouldn't mind,' she said. 'Sister Faith likes you and we can do her gently and without fuss.'

Rebecca ran from the building through the fine drizzle, hoping she could change without being flustered. I'm late, she thought, but found she had only spent ten minutes with Sister Faith, and had plenty of time. Her hair hung down in a glowing roll of heavy silkiness and she decided to leave it down. The dress slipped on easily and she changed her tights for ones of pale pink with tiny roses up the sides that picked out the tone of her high-heeled pink shoes. The necklace was perfect, and she hesitated as she held the butterfly first as a brooch on one shoulder and then against her hair, where it looked like an exotic thing with life of its own, just perched for a second on the thick tresses.

She pinned it to her shoulder, deciding it was too glamorous to wear in her hair unless they went some-where really special, but she put the hair fitment in her small evening purse in case she decided to change it in a ladies' room if the occasion called for it.

'*Damn!*' she muttered. The photos still stood on her desk and she was ready to go out. She looked at her watch and then peered out into the darkness. The rain had stopped, but she still had to walk along the damp path to meet Paul, and if he was ready there wouldn't be time to collect the folder and bring it back to the hostel.

She picked up her jacket of fake fur and decided to leave yet another message for Mr Brent at the main desk. He can collect it himself, she thought. I'll have done what I can for him, and when she went through the doors of the private wing again, she wrote a memo for him and left it with the girl behind the desk.

'Going out with Mr Brent?' asked the girl, with an envious glance at the purple dress.

'Mr Brent? Of course not,' said Rebecca sharply. 'Why did you say that?'

'He came in five minutes ago, all dressed up and looking out of this world! Lucky girl. He collected his messages and ran up to your wing for something, then came down very pleased with himself, holding some snaps.'

'I'm glad they caught up with him at last,' said Rebecca. 'I left a message earlier, but I missed him.'

'He said he wanted them to pass on to someone tonight, and went off, smiling,' the girl told her.

Rebecca waited in the foyer, looking out into the darkness that was suddenly stabbed by headlights, but she waited until the lights were dimmed and Paul came in to see if she was there. She was not going out into the damp unless he called for her, she had decided. Why should he sit in the car and expect her to come to him? It was a surprise to Rebecca that she should take this action, or rather to leave the action to him, and even more of a surprise to Paul, who came in looking faintly annoyed.

'Oh, there you are, Becky,' he said.

'Waiting for you, Paul,' she told him, and gave him a big smile.

He held her arm as they walked to the car, and she giggled inwardly. It was uneven on the path and Paul hated getting his suede shoes dirty, but another car sent up a spray of wet as it passed, catching his legs as he was on the vulnerable side.

'I have to meet some people and wanted you to be with me as this concerns you,' he told her as soon as they were safe in the car.

'Anyone I know?' she asked.

'No, I doubt if you've met,' he said, staring ahead at the road, and she sensed his embarrassment. 'I wish you'd kept your hair up, Becky.'

'I thought you liked long hair,' she said, recalling a night after a party when Paul had lost his head and told her he loved her, while smoothing the long hair and kissing it.

'I do, but I'd rather you kept that for me, Becky. I hate to see you with other men when you wear it long. Some men might want . . . they might think you're something you're not,' he said primly.

'You think it's too sexy,' said Rebecca, laughing, but glancing at his stony face, she tried to keep the laughter out of her voice. 'I can't wear a veil or stuff my hair up into a cap if I don't wear it as I do on duty, and I have no intention of having it sheared.' She had an awful picture of Anthony Brent advancing on her with garden shears and a wicked gleam in his eye that was almost more than a passing fantasy.

'It's beautiful,' Paul admitted, 'but after we're married, it might be wise to have it cut.'

'After we're what? Is this a proposal, Paul?' She was shaken. He couldn't take her for granted as much as that, surely? He had said he loved her on more than one occasion, but only hinted at anything more than a relationship that might amuse both of them.

'You knew I wanted you,' he said as if she had insulted him.

'But suddenly you want to marry me and go into retirement. What shall it be, Paul? A house in the country wearing jumpers and pearls and sensible shoes and living with great hairy dogs while you have a flat in town?'

'The country, yes, but no hairy dogs, and I shall be there.'

'You've made plans?' Rebecca asked with a sense of panic.

'You'll hear all about it tonight.' Paul was smiling now. 'I know you'll fit in beautifully, and they'll be very impressed.'

'Fit in? Who are they?' But the car had stopped outside a glossy new restaurant that Rebecca had seen advertised in one of the magazines left by Mrs Baxter. She smiled. Paul would come away hungry. There had been a picture of a lovely plate decorated with four thin slices of avocado pear and five mange-tout peas in a puddle of green sauce made from spinach. That might have been just a starter, but the other dishes certainly weren't very substantial.

The interior was very much an interior decorator's dream with no expense spared, and the clientele matched, with women dressed in expensive clothes accompanied by smooth-looking yuppies.

'We'll have an aperitif,' said Paul, seeming relieved that the rest of the party had yet to arrive, so he
ordered gin and tonic without asking Rebecca what she
would like, and sat watching the door of the cocktail
lounge.

'I'd like to know what's in your mind, Paul,' she
ventured.

'I've bought a big part of the Hawthorne Spa and two
of the other backers are meeting us here tonight, whom I
want you to meet. They know about you and think it's a
very good idea that you should run the nursing side of
the place with me as consultant and one dietician. In
time,' Paul went on, his eyes glinting with enthusiasm,
'we could build on more and more and have a really big
concern.'

'And long hair wouldn't do,' she said, regarding him
over the top of her glass.

'It wouldn't do at all,' he agreed. 'I want you to mingle
but not to be too obvious. No uniform, but more of a
hostess than a nursing officer.'

'And play bridge with all those fat old men? And
swim with them and tell them how well they're doing?'
Rebecca's anger mounted and she shook her head so
that the wonderful swathe of hair rippled in a cloud and
her cheeks were pink. She looked up and saw a man
watching her. He held a small folder in one hand and
with the other he was piloting a pretty girl dressed in blue
who seemed to want to stay.

The expression of distaste on the face of Anthony
Brent might have been because he hated women with
long hair, or it could have been that he had met the girl
on her invitation and it wasn't his scene. As soon as he
saw that Rebecca had recognised him, he turned away,
but not before she had seen his disgust at the opulence

and falseness of the place, a feeling that matched her own.

Why not run to him and push the girl aside? Why not suggest that they go away to a simpler place where they could be surrounded by real people and eat real food? She blushed at the thought and clutched her purse tightly. I'm going mad, she thought. All this isn't happening.

'I'd like you to meet Selim Refet and Monsieur Roger Dupois, our business associates,' said Paul. He coughed gently, and Selim Refet managed to take his gaze away from Rebecca for just long enough to accept the drink offered him.

CHAPTER THREE

'AND YOU really want to go back?' Nurse Frost looked at Sister Faith as if she was mad.

'Of course. That's my work and I'm needed,' said the nun simply. 'But I shall have to be patient and be really fit before I leave England. Nobody is of use if they're ill and take up the valuable time of the others there.'

'At the rate you're recovering, you'll leave here in a week or so,' said Rebecca. 'Mr Brent is taking out your drainage tube today, and your temperature has settled well.'

Sister Faith took the tall glass of water that Nurse Frost had left ready for her, and Rebecca watched, fascinated. The water was cold and clear, but only tap water, yet Sister Faith sipped it as if savouring a fine wine. She drained the glass and Nurse Frost poured more.

'Thank you, Nurse. You've no idea how wonderful that water tastes, and to have as much as I want is a luxury I haven't enjoyed for months.'

'But surely you have water where you work?' Nurse Frost stared at her.

'There's drought in Ethiopia and the Sudan,' said Rebecca. 'I saw a film showing a lot of the riverbeds and wadis dried up, and people from Europe digging wells to try and save the people living there.'

'Then you know what I mean,' said Sister Faith. 'All our water has to be boiled or treated with purifying tablets before we can even clean our teeth.'

Nurse Frost took away the damp towels and soapdish and screwed the top back on the surgical spirit bottle after rubbing the thin back and pressure points of the woman still confined to bed, then she left Rebecca to chart the progress made in the last day or so.

The wing was quiet, with the two post-ops still in Recovery and not expected back for another day. Both fairly strong men were heavy smokers and needed careful supervision, with all the facilities of intensive care ready in case of collapse. Rebecca watched the woman on the bed who had seemed so weak but needed no extra care. She exuded a gentle determination to get well quickly and be back in the heat and dust and squalor of the refugee camps.

'Where exactly is your Mission?' asked Rebecca.

'It's about ten miles from the border with Ethiopia and three hundred miles from Khartoum, the capital. We were a simple group helping local people, until the great drought began and hundreds of starving people came across the border and completely swamped our resources. There was little food and less water, and we had so many children dying that it all seemed hopeless, until people like VSO and the various charities came to help and set up camps.'

'Is there much disease?' asked Rebecca.

'All the usual conditions one finds in such countries, but the worst is malnutrition and water-borne diseases, like hepatitis and Guinea Worm and some eye conditions. We give injections and food and drink and more of the children now survive, but we badly need more helpers to cope, perhaps for three months at a time to set up a camp and to instruct the better educated about treating water and giving out supplies as they come to the camps.'

'There's been so much help given and so many people going out there that surely the problem is getting less?' said Rebecca. The quiet eyes disturbed her, and she felt a sense of personal guilt that she was doing nothing to help.

'We need more skilled people, and our group has a team of four or six doctors, nurses and engineers who come for a few months and then change with another similar group for the same period. They also bring us vital supplies of medicine that might be lost in the general distribution.' Sister Faith smiled. 'It's miraculous what can be brought in one big truck and a Range Rover, and we do have a new well of brackish water that isn't teeming with bacteria. So we purify that with tablets.' She reached for the glass of water again and drank almost greedily. 'I shall miss this more than anything,' she said.

Rebecca walked slowly back to the clinical room and prepared a dressing trolley in case one of the surgeons wanted to inspect a wound. Mr Brent had not been near the wing except at night after she was off duty. He checked Sister Faith and his simple hernia case, but now two of his were in intensive care and he had no need to visit the private wing. He might come today. He did leave a message that he'd take out the drainage tube, she thought, and she sterilised drainage tubes of various sizes in case he needed to insert a smaller one if he felt the wound needed to be left open for a few more days.

Sister Faith's eyes haunted her and the sweet voice seemed to reproach her. Rebecca closed the small steriliser and impatiently tossed her plastic apron into the bin. Playing on her emotions and charity was a kind of moral blackmail. I give to charity, she told herself. I'm doing a vital job where I am and, after all those years of training, haven't I deserved something of the good life? But she couldn't forget the dinner date she had endured with Paul. Endured was the right word, she decided grimly. First there was Selim Refet, making her feel as if his eyes stripped her naked, and the Frenchman making flattering remarks in French that she pretended not to understand, and not least Paul, who so badly wanted to impress the two wealthy men with her beauty and efficiency and the fact that he was a man of the world.

They had ordered from the long and complicated menu and Paul was handed the wine list.

'I think a white wine, well chilled,' he said, and the others nodded as if it wasn't important. He went through the wine list carefully, making the wine waiter hover for what seemed like ages. He also insisted on calling the wine waiter 'sommelier', which while correct did little to impress the Frenchman at the table.

Rebecca grew more and more annoyed and embarrassed, as the other two men obviously couldn't care less about the food but would rather have her for the first course! She wished with all her heart that she had worn a simple sweater and skirt and had left her hair severely pinned in a French pleat.

As the evening wore on, Paul drank more, and when the second bottle arrived, he sampled it and then sent it back, complaining loudly that it was not the right temperature. All the time Rebecca had thought of the tiny woman lying so still, perhaps dreaming of life-giving water of whatever temperature she could give to her flock.

It was late when they walked out to the car and Paul sank into the driver's seat. Rebecca sat stiffly, scared that he would drive too fast, bump into something or be caught and breathalised, but they reached the Princess

Beatrice safely and she slipped out of her side of the car before Paul could kiss her. 'It's very late,' she said. 'I have to make an early start as we have surgical cases tomorrow.'

Paul opened his door and pulled himself out.

'C'mon, Becky, it isn't every night a man asks a girl to marry him.'

'You *told* me, you mean,' she replied with some heat. 'You told me a number of things, and I want none of it, Paul. I have no intention of leaving this hospital, and I don't want to marry you.'

'Becky darling,' he whispered, 'don't say that! You know I love you, and after the way those two were eyeing you tonight, I must make sure you're mine.' He lurched towards her and grabbed her arm, bringing her roughly into a tight embrace. 'Darling Becky, I'll never let you go,' he said. He kissed her cheeks and tried to reach her lips, but she struggled away. His hand clutched at her hair and forced her to face his kiss. 'That hair . . . you're right, you must never cut it, but save it for me when we're alone.'

Desperately she pushed him away, revolted. How had she once thought it possible to marry this man if he asked her? Apart from his drunken, moist kisses, he had shown clearly that he was only in medicine for the money it would make for him, and wanted her to stoop to his level.

Rebecca was free and turned to run to the path leading to the hostel. Paul called after her, but didn't follow, and she ran breathless through the wet leaves and darkness sobbing as she tried to catch her breath. Her small evening purse was difficult to open and she fumbled for the key, half afraid that Paul might change his mind and come after her. The door was locked after midnight and she knew she had her key somewhere. A light over the porch helped her and she bent once more to look in her bag, but a hand already holding a key slipped past her and the key turned smoothly in the lock.

Anthony Brent pushed the door wide and stepped back. His manner was correct and his face expressionless, and Rebecca walked thankfully into the hall. She turned to make sure that the door was shut and locked again, and gave a sigh of relief.

'Did the bears get you?' asked the man who now stood regarding her with a half-smile.

'No.' Rebecca gulped and pushed a hand through her dishevelled hair. 'I'm afraid of the dark,' she lied.

'He isn't coming here,' said Anthony Brent. 'He had second thoughts. Perhaps he also is afraid of the dark —or of you, Sister Perivale.'

'That's a private matter,' she said, and tried to do up the stubborn zip on her purse, but she knew it had caught on the fabric that lined the bag. She tugged and her key shot on to the floor, with her lipstick, a few coins and the fixture for her brooch.

They bent to pick up the scattered items and Anthony Brent found the silver pin and attachment. He sat on the bench by the telephone and turned it over in his hands. 'Curious,' he remarked. 'Now could it be some secret weapon for ladies afraid of the dark? Could it be something nasty for use as a toothpick, an ear-scrape, or what?'

'It's a hairpin,' said Rebecca. She was regaining her poise and had stuffed the other things back in the bag except for her room key. She held out her hand for the pin.

'Not very decorative,' he remarked, and made no attempt to give it back.

'It fixes to a butterfly,' she said, and laughed at his expression. 'Not a real one.' She slipped her jacket down from her shoulders and it fell on to the seat. The brooch glowed softly and he touched it, following the lines of the wings and the antennae.

'My mother had one set with rubies,' he said, as if he had forgotten the girl wearing it.

'Had?' she queried. 'What happened to it?'

'She was in an accident from which she never recovered and the brooch disappeared at the time. That one had no hairpin, it was just a brooch,' he said, as if the past must never be recalled. 'Show me,' he demanded, and Rebecca unpinned the brooch and handed it to him.

'It's exquisite,' he said, and unscrewed the pin, replacing it with the hairpin. 'Exquisite,' he said again, and Rebecca closed her eyes as he smoothed back her hair and placed the butterfly to one side where the long strands of silk fell thickest. The touch was light and yet it held a deep caress. The smell of a healthy male and good aftershave made her lips tremble, and the sensation of his lips, warm and full and tender on hers for just a butterfly kiss, made her helpless.

She opened her eyes and saw a pain mixed with anger in his face.

'I'm sorry,' he said quietly. 'It stirred a few memories.' She saw him stride away and then put a hand to her hair. The butterfly hung loosely and she removed it, pulling at her hair until it brought tears to her eyes.

But the tears were there when she unlocked her room door, and they were there while she undressed and brushed out her hair. There was so much that she could have and didn't want, and so much she wanted and couldn't have! She placed the butterfly carefully in the velvet-lined box and slipped it to the back of her top

drawer. I shall never wear it again, she thought. One
kiss, one touch, and it's now something special, rare and
infinitely sad.

'Mr Brent's here, Sister!' called Nurse Frost, and
Rebecca was startled out of her dream. She instinctively
put a hand to the sleek folds under her cap, as if she
might find it down in a cloud with a butterfly hovering
over it. She walked along to Sister Faith's room and
asked the junior to bring the trolley.

'You can gown and mask and watch, Nurse,' said
Rebecca. The girl flushed with pleasure. 'Just hand me
anything you're asked for, but keep away from the
trolley and the bed and don't make a sound,' she went
on, glad to have something to take her mind off the man
she must face in a few seconds.

Sister Faith was lying propped up on several pillows,
and her eyes sparkled. 'No, I'm not afraid, Mr Brent.
This is another step forward, please God, and soon I
shall be as good as new.'

'You could have a whiff of something to take the edge
off,' he told her, 'but I prefer to use a local anaesthetic
spray as there's only one deep stitch that might be
painful.'

'If that's the one that pulls when I sit up, then I shall be
glad to see it go,' Sister said firmly.

Rebecca put on a mask and handed one to each of the
others in the room. She folded back the bedclothes to
reveal just the scar and the drainage incision, and when
Mr Brent had scrubbed at the vanitory unit in the corner
of the room, she took the sterile towel off the trolley and
he helped himself to swabs and lotion, then took the
rubber drain carefully in forceps before feeling down to

the one stitch that held it inside the wound. Rebecca watched the face on the pillow, and hoped the brief spray of local had numbed the part sufficiently, but Sister Faith gave no sign that she was in any pain and he withdrew the tacky drain and threw it in the dish that the junior held as if it was the Holy Grail.

A spurt of discharge followed the drain, and the tube into the bottle of disinfectant gurgled as the junior nurse took it away to the sluice room. Anthony Brent pressed round the wound, watching Sister Faith's face all the time. There was no deep discomfort, and he inserted a length of sterile gauze dipped in aqueous flavine into the gap in the skin left by the drain.

He turned and for the first time looked at Rebecca, who stood holding a corset-dressing which would allow the wound to be inspected and dressed without having to pull away adhesive plaster every time. 'Good,' he said quietly. 'I was wondering how we could avoid making the skin sore.' He watched Rebecca's deft fingers and then felt the pulse in the not-so-emaciated wrist.

'You've done very well, Sister Faith,' he said, and the admiration in his voice made Rebecca feel slightly envious. There was no passion in his voice, nor could there be for someone like Sister Faith, but there was warmth and respect and real affection, not just a fleeting moment of attraction like the flight of a butterfly.

'When may I go back?' the nun asked eagerly.

'First some physiotherapy and exercise to get some tone back into your muscles, and we must feed you well. Another week here and a few weeks at the Convent and then a final check.' He laughed. 'I may have you under my wing until I too leave here!'

Rebecca froze. She had forgotten that he was working

at Beattie's for such a short time. Another six weeks or so and she would never see him again.

'I've been trying to convince Sister Perivale that she would be welcome in the Sudan,' said Sister Faith.

Anthony Brent regarded the slim arms and small hands of the wing Sister and smiled. 'You have to be really tough out there, Sister Perivale. Lots of heat, bugs, and the nights are very, very dark. I have female relatives who are doctors and they're strong and able to do such work, but I doubt if you'd stick it for a couple of weeks.'

There was a challenge in his eyes and a hint of amused condescension that made Rebecca blush. She clenched her hands and tried to appear unmoved. 'All my family are finely made,' she said sweetly. 'Small but strong, built for speed and service and not like lumbering carthorses.'

'Oh, dear,' he said, with mock concern, 'I must remember to tell my sisters your opinion!'

Sister Faith looked amused. 'If I didn't know what good people you are, I'd think you were fighting,' she commented.

'We don't know each other well enough for that,' said Rebecca, and smoothed the duvet and pillows before taking away the two vases of flowers that Nurse Frost had 'won' from a patient going home. 'I'll bring them back when I've taken out the dead ones,' she said, and left Mr Brent to take the notes back to the office when he had finished talking to Sister Faith, but ten minutes later he was still inside the room, and Rebecca glanced at the door and wondered uneasily if they were talking about her.

She answered the telephone and was told that Mr Johns, the patient who had been in intensive care after a long session in the theatre for removal of part of his gut, was ready to return to the wing for further nursing, and would she inform Mr Brent if he was in the wing?

Rebecca tapped on the door and opened it. Sister Faith was nibbling at a biscuit and Mr Brent was drinking coffee. She looked at them and then at the tray on the bed table.

'It's all right, Sister. I asked the little nurse to bring us our coffee now as I wanted to talk to Sister Faith and I haven't time to waste,' said Anthony Brent.

There was no real reason to feel annoyed. Patients were due for morning coffee and many of the consultants had coffee wherever they happened to be working, but he did take it for granted that he could give orders in her department, and Rebecca felt snubbed.

'If I'd known you weren't busy, I'd have asked for some more for you,' he said, and smiled.

'I am busy. They rang down from Intensive Care and Mr Johns will be here in half an hour. Just to let you know,' she said, and left them again.

She looked at the off-duty schedule and saw that Nurse Frost had a half day off before her day off, so if she wanted any leisure, Rebecca knew she must go off soon and be back in the wing to relieve her, after lunch.

She waited until the patient was comfortable in bed and saw that all his notes were complete, the right drugs had come with him and his chart was made up and showed a great improvement in his condition, then Nurse Frost took the keys and Rebecca walked over to her room.

She looked in the slot marked P and found two letters for her, and there was a pile of medical journals on the table in the entrance foyer for one of the doctors. She looked at the board where telephone messages were often put if someone answered the phone and couldn't find the person the caller wanted. She stared.

'Mr Brent to ring Meryl Sachs, urgently,' she read on one of the pink slips. A number was scribbled after the message. On the next slip was a message for her, and she took it from the clip and tore it up. Paul knew she would be off duty this morning, and the message said he would meet her in the Falcon for a pub lunch at twelve.

Rebecca went slowly up to her room. Paul was crafty enough to know that in her present mood she would have hung up on him if he rang her directly, but it was difficult to ignore a message like this and keep him waiting alone in the pub the medical and nursing staff of Beattie's used as a very convenient and comfortable watering hole.

She changed from uniform into the green suede skirt and a shirt of pale yellow under the matching suede bomber jacket, pulled on thick amber tights and thrust her feet into glossy brown Robin Hood boots. She left her hair firmly pinned in its neat style and picked up a velvet cap that matched her tights in colour.

I'll go down the hill to the boutique first, she decided, then take the bus up to the Falcon. I have to eat somewhere, and maybe it's time I talked to Paul in neutral surroundings where he can't raise his voice or make a grab at me!

A thin glimpse of sunlight through the last of the sad leaves hanging on the outer twigs of the trees in the drive encouraged her. The rain had stopped at last and it might even be a fine day for Nurse Frost tomorrow when she went to meet her fiancé. Rebecca picked up the brown leather tote bag and made sure that both the keys were in the inner purse before going slowly down the stairs, thinking about what shopping she ought to do while she was in the small row of shops and stalls down the road.

In the hall, she paused to look at the illustration on the front cover of *The New Scientist*, a journal she often borrowed from Anne Downer, the house surgeon on Women's Medical, and as she put it on the table, the front door opened and Anthony Brent came in. He glanced at the board and snatched the pink memo slip. He swore softly under his breath when he saw the time the message had been received and turned to find the telephone.

Rebecca stood aside as once more she was in danger of being knocked over by his impetuous movement, and he saw who was standing by the table as if she had all day to spare, dressed for a date.

'Did you see this when you came over?' he demanded.

'Yes,' she said. 'I always look on the board. I wondered if I should ring the wing to tell you, but I was sure that by now you would have left and might even be on your way here.'

'You might have tried,' he said coldly. 'That message says urgent, and when she says urgent, that's exactly what she means! Move over, I must use the phone.'

Rebecca bent to pick up her bag as the dialling tone sounded. Before she reached the door, she heard him say, 'Thank God you haven't left, I know you're pressed for time, but I must see you!'

She walked slowly down the drive and out through the wide gateway between the huge wrought-iron gates that were seldom closed and had seen so much of drama, joy and sorrow pass that way, to and from the hospital that cared for the families in the big houses and in the rooms in the Peabody Buildings alike.

She ignored the cheery wave from the lodge, where Claud, the porter, watched everything and missed nothing, and stopped only when she was staring into the window of the new boutique, seeing nothing, aware of only one thing, that Anthony Brent cared deeply for a woman called Meryl Sachs and was rushing to meet her . . . just once more for a lovers' meeting, hating to lose her, wherever she might be going.

By half past eleven she had finished her shopping and stood by the bus stop that would take her up the hill, past the hospital again and round to the Falcon. A car swept by going in the direction of the city, and in it she saw the tense face of Anthony Brent, driving with care but as fast as he dared. From the set of his shoulders and the eagerness of his expression, she thought of only his need and haste to reach a woman who must mean a lot to him.

Was the photograph of the pretty girl a clue to this meeting? A girl with short hair, smiling and looking at ease with the handsome surgeon and in just a simple white shirtwaister dress, had his full attention.

Curiosity more than any desire to have lunch with Paul now made her anxious to get to the Falcon on time, and when the bus set her down by the corner she hurried to the Merlin Bar where she knew Paul would find her.

'You look good,' he said, kissing her cheek in greeting. 'I wish you'd do your hair like that all the time, in public. You've no idea what havoc you caused with Selim and Monsieur Dupois the other evening!'

'I thought you wanted to show me off as one of your assets,' she said, with a hint of irony that seemed to slide off him.

'I admit they seem even more anxious now to do business with me, and I have the agreement signed, and now I must go down and find out what needs to be done. When do you have a weekend free?'

'Next week,' she said, 'but I've arranged to visit friends in Brighton and stay with an old school friend who used to be a nurse but gave it up to get married.'

'You can make some excuse,' said Paul. 'I need you at the Hawthorne to go over the medical equipment and the gymnasium.'

'If I'm to eat here, we must go in,' said Rebecca. 'I have to get back to relieve Nurse Frost.' She tried to sound relaxed, but inwardly she was fuming. We shall either have a blistering row or I must keep quiet, she realised. 'I'm afraid my arrangement stands, Paul,' she said as soon as they sat down to eat the well-cooked lasagne that the Falcon served. She took some salad and shook her head when Paul offered her a drink. 'Just a mineral water, or I'll fall asleep this afternoon,' she said.

She sipped the ice-cold Perrier and thought of Sister Faith. I can't waste my life at the Hawthorne Spa, or at least not until I finish acute nursing and want to mark time, she thought.

'How do you get on with Brent?' asked Paul bluntly.

'He's excellent in the theatre, I believe, and his patients do very well,' said Rebecca evenly. It was an effort not to start when his name was mentioned, but she wanted to find out more about him. 'I don't know much about him,' she said with polite interest. 'Bart's, isn't he?'

'Yes, but not for a year now. He went off to one of the third world countries as a consultant and I think he may go back there.' Paul glanced at her. 'I hope you don't have to see him too often—I saw the look he gave you when I first met him.'

'Don't be silly, Paul! He was in a raging temper and not in the mood for leering at the staff,' said Rebecca lightly. 'You imagine it. You imagine that Selim and his friend are lusting after me, too, and I'm sure it's all in your mind.' Her heart beat faster. They say the onlooker sees more of the game, she thought, then dismissed it as just another sign of Paul's possessiveness, but her hand crept up to her hair where the butterfly clip had rested. Such a brief touch, a kiss that wasn't really a kiss and a long, cool look at her in the restaurant when her face was flushed and her hair loose. That was all she had to remember and all she would ever have.

'Brighton is quite close to the Hawthorne, so you can do both. I'll drive you down to your friend and pick you up on Sunday morning to see the Hawthorne, then we'll drive back later and have a meal on the way.'

It all sounded so reasonable, and Rebecca could think of no excuse to refuse, as this would cut out a boring coach trip or train journey and actually save time.

'I must go,' she said, and Paul got up reluctantly to drive her back.

'We haven't talked about us,' he said.

'Let's leave it,' she begged. 'I'll see the Hawthorne and then we'll talk.' The crowded bar of the Falcon was no place to argue, and she dreaded having to make him believe that she was in earnest.

Paul nodded to one or two colleagues as they pushed a way to the door and smiled at the knowing glances from people who thought he and Rebecca were lovers, and he was in a good mood as he drove her back to the hospital, leaving her in the front car park to walk along the path to the hostel.

She glanced at the notice board as she went in, and saw another slip with her name on it. Rebecca gasped, then frowned. The nerve of the man! She had given him no encouragement, and yet Selim Refet had telephoned her. The phone shrilled and she put out a hand to answer it, then nearly dropped it as if it might sting her.

'Hello, Becky,' came the smooth voice. Rebecca

winced. Few people called her Becky unless they knew her very well, and this man had no right to use it.

'Who is that?' she asked coldly, but she had no doubt that it was the good-looking Egyptian.

'I wondered when we could meet,' he said. 'There will be so much to discuss about our project, and it needs the ideas and expertise of a woman.'

'Oh, it's Mr Refet!' she said with an air of surprise. 'I expect we shall meet soon. I have to go to the Hawthorne with Paul next weekend and we shall see you then.'

'I thought perhaps dinner tonight,' he said.

'I'm sorry, I'm on duty and then on call,' she told him, stretching the truth a little. 'It will have to be next weekend,' she added, and put down the phone.

She turned. 'Oh, did you get through to your caller?' she asked. Anthony Brent was watching her and Rebecca knew she was pink-cheeked and that her eyes must show the annoyance she felt over her call.

'Yes, thank you,' he said, and walked away. She saw a pink slip in his hand that had been torn and knew that he had picked it up, smoothed it out and read it. Her colour deepened. So now he thinks I'm planning a weekend with Selim Refet! Ah well, what does it matter? He's never going to fall in love with me, so he can think I'm having an affair with Paul and a bit on the side with Selim. Why should I care? But as she dressed for duty, her eyes were hot with unshed tears and her heart was heavy.

If only I could get away from everyone, she thought. The smell of the sluice and the sight of the used dressing trolley waiting to be cleared in the clinical room was suddenly distasteful. The sound of laughter from two women cleaning the corridor shut her out into her own misery, and Nurse Frost went off duty, beaming with anticipation of a wonderful weekend.

Sister Faith was asleep and the two new cases were very demanding, one asking for more and more pain-killers until Rebecca began to suspect he had a drug problem that had nothing to do with pain relief. More flowers came from the florist down the road, an agent for an international floral delivery service, and she knew just how expensive the arrangements were. Two fresh sheafs of lovely Riviera carnations sat on the shelf by her office, left by one of the patients discharged that day and wilting in the heat of the radiator.

Rebecca plunged the stems of the flowers into cold water, then arranged them in pretty vases. The scent was heavy and sweet, and she closed her eyes as she buried her face in the fragrance. She put one vase in her office and the other in Sister Faith's room when she went to see if the nun was ready to walk with help along the corridor and back.

'Such progress!' smiled Sister Faith. 'I had physio this morning and feel much stronger. I'm sure I can walk about on my own now, Sister.'

'I have the time to help if you need me, and please don't do too much, as it should be a gradual increase each day, not a marathon,' said Rebecca, laughing and delighted that the nun was so much better.

'Women in greater pain than I walk for miles in the hot sun to our clinic,' said Sister Faith. 'Women who've been mutilated by village midwives when they're circumcised.'

'But I thought it was an archaic practice that they've abandoned!' exclaimed Rebecca, horrified.

'It's very widespread, and it's a part of our work to educate these people and try to stop it. All these things have to be pushed aside when there's such an immediate problem of malnutrition and sickness, but I hope we can go back to our programme soon.'

'They must have help,' said Rebecca.

'People like you, who could give up a job for a few months and come back to it after a stint in the Third World,' said Sister Faith.

'You really want me to volunteer, don't you?' said Rebecca uneasily. 'I don't think I'd be of much use.'

'We think you would,' said Sister Faith. 'You go abroad on holiday, so why not extend that with service?'

'You'd have to tell me how, and what jabs I'd need.'

The power of the frail woman was overwhelming and Rebecca felt almost hypnotised. Why not go? she thought. It would solve a lot of problems and give me time to think. I could do some good and come back to whatever I decide is my future—with Paul, working in this unit again or back to midwifery.

'I would have to give a month's notice and make sure I'd be welcome to come back to my job,' she ventured.

'You'll need that for inoculations and visas,' said Sister Faith. 'But leave it to me to arrange. Just give in your notice tomorrow, and trust me.'

CHAPTER FOUR

'YOU CAN'T do this to me!' Paul nearly shouted the words, and Rebecca pedalled faster on the cycling machine in the spa gymnasium. 'You can't swan off to Africa now when I need you here!'

'This clock isn't right, I'm sure,' said Rebecca calmly. 'I'll try the treadmill next.'

'Come here, and be serious!'

'You asked me to test all the apparatus, and that's what I'm doing.' She pressed the switch and began to walk the mill, glad to have strenuous exercise to rid her of her tensions. 'This is good. You should try it, Paul.'

Breathless, she switched off and stood by the wall bars.

'Not that!' groaned Paul. 'You made me tired just watching you!'

'I like to try all the amenities, even if we can't guarantee that your two friends will have a massage parlour as an extra, unless they have massage from that beefy woman in the shower area!'

Paul went red. 'That was an unfortunate misunderstanding,' he said. 'They didn't mean to insult you.'

'Misunderstanding? I understood perfectly, Paul, and it only made me more determined that I want nothing to do with this venture!' Rebecca pulled on her zipper-jacket and dabbed her hot face with a tissue. 'I could use a shower, but not here. I'd be scared of those creeps coming in and catching me in the nuddie!'

'Be reasonable,' he said, with real emotion, and he

repeated it several times on the way back to London, but Rebecca felt strangely elated and knew she had made a wise decision. In five weeks' time she would be on her way to Khartoum and then on to the camp, with all her inoculation certificates signed and her visa valid for unpaid work in the Sudan.

'We feed you and give you enough local currency for things like toothpaste and other necessities, but you get no real salary,' Sister Faith explained. 'We pay for the simplest forms of travel and you bring your own clothes and suitable white coats if you think they're useful, but keep luggage to a minimum, as every cubic foot in the Land Rover or truck is precious and must be used for vital supplies.'

'I can manage,' said Rebecca. 'I've earned quite a lot here and I have some money of my own, so when I come back I shan't be destitute.'

'I'm sure you won't,' said Sister Faith. 'There'll always be a friend somewhere caring for you.' She laughed softly. 'You're blessed, Rebecca, and I see great happiness ahead for you.'

'It will bring a certain satisfaction, I suppose,' Rebecca admitted.

'That's not what I had in mind entirely,' the nun replied, and went on to suggest suitable clothes and equipment to take to a hot climate.

'I bought a huge mug as you suggested, Sister,' said Rebecca one day. 'It was difficult to get one that wasn't plastic, but I managed to find a real Boy Scout effort in an army surplus store that I can put on heat if necessary. What about a mosquito net? The man tried to sell me one, but I thought I'd ask you first.'

'We have some in the store, but now the weather is so dry we have no need for them, as mosquitoes breed in water and we have none. If the rains come, then you must be sure to take anti-malarial pills and sleep under a net, but I doubt if we shall have that problem yet.'

There was so much to do and to think about that Rebecca had no time to think of Paul or his problems, and it was good to be able to push all thoughts of Anthony Brent from her mind. She saw very little of him now as he came at night for his round and had no beds available for surgical cases, and even Sister Faith needed nothing from him, with her wound healed and her health improved and her one small bag packed in readiness for a week or so at the Convent.

'I shall miss you,' said Rebecca as she went down to the taxi with Sister Faith.

'We shall meet again soon.' Sister Faith took her hand. 'You'll make new friends and meet some familiar faces. Never scorn any friendship, Rebecca. Even Paul has given you something, if only the spur to come out to Africa.'

'I can't think of anyone I know who's likely to turn up out there,' Rebecca said shakily. 'I may be all alone.'

'Wait and see, and God bless you,' said Sister Faith, and stepped with surprising briskness into the car.

'Has she left?' asked Anthony Brent, later.

'This afternoon,' said Rebecca, and winced slightly. The last injection for cholera had not been comfortable, and her arm ached.

'I hear you're joining the great adventure,' he remarked, and sat on the edge of the desk as if he had all the time in the world to spare.

'If having needles stuck in me is adventure, I've joined!' she replied with feeling.

'I said you hadn't the physique for it,' he said heartlessly, and grinned.

'I'm strong enough! I've nursed athletes who were huge and very butch, and they fainted at the sight of a needle,' she said. 'Look at Sister Faith. She has more resilience than anyone I know, and she can't wait to be in that awful place. Now she's gone, do you think I can opt out?'

'Not a hope. I shall be in touch and I shall tell her.'

'Sneak,' she said weakly, and suddenly felt very odd.

'Careful!' His arms held her close and he lowered her into her chair. His touch was gentle as he undid the tight collar of her uniform dress and the first two buttons of the front. He buzzed for a nurse and asked briskly for water as Sister Perivale was feeling faint, then smoothed back her hair and found the pulse in her temple. 'Fast but not serious,' he said, and took the glass of water the junior brought and held it to Rebecca's lips. 'You can go, Nurse. Nothing serious, just a reaction to all those jabs,' he said smoothly. 'Ask Nurse Frost to spare me a moment, if she's on duty.' He smiled as if it was a part of his duty to hold the Sister of the private patients' wing in his arms, long after she had sipped the water and now wanted to sit up.

Rebecca felt a wave of warmth flood through her body and a peace that wanted to make her slide back into those wonderful, strong and sensuous arms, but she became conscious of her disturbed uniform dress and knew that under it she wore only a tiny half-bra with a wire base and that he was far too close for modesty. At least he didn't feel my heartbeat, she thought, and colour flooded her cheeks.

'Recovery!' he said, and released her with obvious reluctance. 'Sometimes I think I could have been a good doctor.'

'You are,' she said, and hoped she did up her dress

buttons as if she hadn't noticed his hand lingering on the softness of her throat.

'Why are you going to Africa?' he asked abruptly.

'Sister Faith——' she began.

'Sister Faith gave you the excuse you needed, and your decision was a bit sudden.'

'I wanted a change of scene,' she said lightly. 'I wanted new faces and new experiences.'

'And to get away from anyone in particular?' His face was tense. 'Someone here? It can't be Weldon as he told me that you and he are going into partnership, so I assume you've made it up after your spat a little while ago.' He gave a short laugh. 'Did you think this would be an easy ride, Rebecca? Did you think it might be one last fling before settling down at the Spa?'

'No, that isn't true! You've got it all wrong. I do want to leave here for a while and I do want to help Sister Faith and her refugees, but you could never understand.' Rebecca's voice faded under his dark, stormy gaze. 'We're not . . . you know nothing about me,' she whispered, and glanced up at him.

'I know you aren't made for the rigours you'll have to face out there. I know you should stay here and be as you are, doing a good job in your own sphere and looking beautiful.'

'That isn't enough,' she explained. 'I must fill my heart with simple things, as the poet says.' She smiled wanly. 'You're going away too, I hear. Did she like the photographs?'

'Meryl?' He stared at her. 'I'd forgotten, you did leave a message for me.' He grinned sheepishly. 'I move fast and leave a trail of forgotten thanks behind me, but don't think I haven't enjoyed . . . working with you.'

The pause was slight as if he had searched for words, and then said something that wasn't upmost in his mind.

'You're very good . . . with your patients,' said Rebecca.

His grin became wicked. 'And now you are my patient, until your formidable Nurse Frost brushes me aside and takes charge.' He bent and kissed her on the lips and his eyes lost their laughter. 'We'll meet again, little butterfly,' he told her. 'Look over your shoulder one day and I shall be there.'

'With the girl in the picture?' she asked sadly.

'Probably,' was all he said, and he stood away from her chair as Nurse Frost bustled in anxiously.

'You shouldn't leave here, Sister. Just look at you, all flushed and bright-eyed! I never really trust those inoculations—they have bad side-effects on some people.'

'She's fine, Nurse. A slight raise in pulse, but only temporary, I assure you,' Anthony Brent said smoothly. He picked up his notes from the desk. 'I shall see you before you leave, Sister.'

'You both leave at about the same time, don't you?' asked Nurse Frost.

'Morton is coming back,' said Mr Brent, as if that was explanation enough.

'I heard you'd been in Africa,' Nurse Frost went on. 'Once was enough, I should think! Bart's and the West End must seem heaven after that.'

'Once was quite an experience,' he agreed. He looked at Rebecca. 'An experience in many ways, but it's never possible to escape life or people or beliefs out there. They have a habit of cropping up when you least expect them.'

Rebecca smiled when he had gone, and Nurse Frost

was convinced that her wing Sister wasn't dying. Paul was hardly likely to 'crop up' in Africa, and Anthony Brent would be far too busy with his Meryl to leave England.

We might meet casually when I come back, she thought. One day, as he said, I shall look up and see him there, and he'll absentmindedly ask if I've been away! She took the two codeine tablets that Mr Brent had suggested and a long drink of water. The sensation of walking on foam with her head cut off at the scalp receded and she was able to get on with her duties, and by the time she was back on the wing after a heavy sleep all night, she felt energetic enough to finish her shopping in the West End, and to enjoy her day off, with an excitement mingled with awe that she would be leaving London, leaving her friends and leaving the two men who each made life so difficult.

Four thin cotton dresses of Liberty print would take up very little room in her pack, and bikini pants and bras were wisps of silk and cotton that could be pushed in anywhere. A linen hat that Sister Faith said would fold up and be more portable than straw until she reached Africa, and various other light clothes such as shorts and long-sleeved shirts and a pair of cotton trousers, seemed all that was needed. She decided against uniform of any kind and put in two or three aprons and one of plastic.

Even with her load reduced as much as possible her rucksack was bulky and she was glad that a heavy mosquito net was unnecessary. The huge mug hung rather selfconsciously on the strap of the pack and she also had her own knife, fork and spoon, as if, as Nurse Frost said, you're going to a Girl Guide camp.

'I shall take light shoes and wear those horrible safari boots that everyone seems to wear out there,' said

Rebecca when she had re-packed for the third time under Maeve's watchful eye.

'You don't want nasties boring between your toes and giving you sleeping sickness,' said Maeve, making herself comfortable on the bed and eating a melting choc-ice she had stored in the ward fridge until she came off duty. 'Dress like Princess Anne out there and you can't go wrong. She wears long-sleeved shirts and chukka boots all the time she visits the Third World.'

'It does make sense,' agreed Rebecca. 'A lot of disease is spread in the dust and insects. Why am I going?' she wailed. 'Paul has left me severely alone, and even those two men who own part of the Hawthorne have given up asking me to dinner. I could pretend I've gone, and find another PP wing here.'

'Like Bart's?' Maeve's dark Celtic eyes sparkled. 'Anthony said he'd be back from leave and concentrate on his cases there. I shall miss him very much. He's a dream to have around in a crisis, and the nurses all adore him.'

'I think he's booked,' said Rebecca. 'What do we know about him?' She tried to sound mildly curious, but Maeve laughed.

'Dying to know, aren't you? Well, your guess is as good as any. He likes you—is that any good? He mentions you often, and I wonder if it's all professional interest.' Maeve folded the ice-cream paper carefully before tossing it into Rebecca's waste basket.

'He finds me attractive, but that's nothing. I've had enough of brushing-off men who think I'm pretty and therefore easy. At least in the bush or whatever they call the land there, I can wear that ghastly hat over my hair screwed up in a bun and perspire gently against a background of sand.'

'Well, don't get too burned. You never know, when he sees you again, he could find he's missed you.'

Rebecca gave her a dirty look and went on trying to get malaria tablets, anti-histamine cream, aspirin and Lomotil into a zipper make-up bag, with safety pins, sticking plaster and antiseptic cream. 'To think that this once held a very expensive selection of Elizabeth Arden beauty products!' she said thoughtfully.

'The supreme sacrifice!' agreed Maeve. 'I'm taking the day off to come to the airport with you,' she announced casually.

'Oh, Maeve, that's wonderful!' Rebecca brushed away a tear. 'I get a fit of the panics sometimes and I might run out on the whole project unless I'm put firmly through passport control.'

'The day after tomorrow,' said Maeve, levering herself off the bed. 'I hate melted ice-cream, it repeats,' she said to hide her own emotion. 'Taxi ordered?' Rebecca nodded. 'I'll come with you and visit my cousin who lives near the airport. They've had double glazing put in, so this time we may be able to hear each other speak.'

'I hate saying goodbye,' said Rebecca.

'You'll be back in six months at the latest, three if you get something bad or can't stand the heat,' said Maeve cheerfully. 'Go back on duty tomorrow and get it over. Then have a good rest and we have an early start. Crack of dawn,' she added. 'And I'm not a lark, I'm a night owl.'

'You've no idea how much it means to have you there,' said Rebecca.

'I like airports,' said Maeve. 'Always I have this feeling that one day I shall be knocked over by a millionaire wheeling one of the trolleys that get out of control and he'll take me away from all this.' She rolled her eyes dramatically. 'Tomorrow it might happen.'

'Idiot!' laughed Rebecca. 'Come to Africa and be abducted by a Sudanese landowner.'

'Have you heard what they do to their women? No, a Texas millionaire will do nicely, thank you.' Maeve left her to stack away all the clothes she wouldn't take with her and to push the cases along to the store at the end of the corridor. She looked round her room, now devoid of all her personal photographs, books and ornaments, and found she had a lump in her throat. The room had been home for her for long enough to make it hers in every sense of the word, and now someone else would live here and when she returned she might have another room.

Nothing is permanent, she decided. It's better to travel light and not put down too many roots that are painful to drag up when I leave. Nurse Frost would be married this time next year and put down roots for good. Rebecca gulped. Out there was the city and beyond it the world across the sea, oceans without end, land limitless, and she was a speck on the globe. She took a deep breath. I'm leaving Paul who would make me have too many strangling roots, leaving something that could never begin, my love for Anthony Brent, and this dear old hospital.

Everything added up to sadness now, and the little presents she received from staff and patients made her want to weep. The sooner I get away, the more settled I'll be, she thought, but the sound of the taxi horn outside the main entrance on the morning she left was like a knell of desolation.

'You have everything?' asked Maeve. Rebecca nodded. 'Passport, visas, inoculation certificates, money?'

'I checked and double-checked,' said Rebecca, 'and I

carried my luggage over here early so that I could make
sure I'd left nothing in my room. I wonder if you'd look
after this for me? I haven't a lot of jewellery, but this box
has one or two things I'd hate to lose, and it's not really
on to wear these in Africa.'

'You'll come back with endless strings of beads and
brass rings round your neck,' said Maeve. She shrugged.
'Maybe not—geography was never my strong point.'

'Whatever is in fashion, I'll bring you some,' said
Rebecca. Her pack was neatly buckled and the small
in-flight bag contained overnight things and toilet
articles in case her main luggage went astray. It also had
a stack of cheap ballpoint pens and cheap combs, as
Sister Faith had said they were in very short supply for
the children.

'Chewing gum!' said Maeve. 'You'll need plenty, and
it's useful to give away. My brother was in the Gulf as an
engineer and swore it saved his life.' She ran to a
machine at the airport and came back with a handful of
packets. 'My goodbye gift, and may your mouth never
go dry.' She tried to laugh. 'I'm getting high on sadness,'
she said, and bought coffee and doughnuts to help pass
the time.

From time to time the Tannoy sent out scrambled
messages, and they strained their ears to find out what
was being said. The rucksack had been swallowed into
the maw of the moving carousel behind the plastic
curtain, and Rebecca held her flight bag and document
case ready to go through Passport Control. The crowd
was dense and she looked back to catch a last glimpse of
Maeve, the last glimpse of someone she knew and liked,
before crossing the barrier into the unknown.

Heads bobbed about and people jostled for place, and
she saw a dark head bent over a case that was so like

Anthony Brent's that she almost shouted his name. He looked up and she knew she was mistaken, but she couldn't say if she was relieved or disappointed. The line of people thinned and she was through the Customs barrier, feeling like a refugee herself. Would it have been easier to have Paul there, waving her goodbye with his now permanent frown when they met? No, I'm glad I didn't tell him I leave today, she thought. It's bad enough like this, without having him make a scene.

The smiling stewardess checked her in to her seat by the window halfway back in the plane, and Rebecca put her flight bag under the seat. The shoulder-bag of plain tan leather that was strong enough to carry more than money and a few necessities now bulged with chewing gum and fruit sweets, and she put her passport away safely.

A woman came to the seat next to her, with a boy of about twelve on the end of the row who peered past his mother to see out of the window. He stared at Rebecca as if he willed her to move and change places, and she could imagine him being a nuisance on the long flight if he didn't have a window seat.

From experience, Rebecca knew they would see a lot of cloud and very little of the land beneath or the ships as they crossed the sea, and the boy was excited at the thrill of travelling by air. 'Would you like to change places?' she asked, and after embarrassed half-refusals from the woman, they changed, and Rebecca had the seat by the aisle.

The take-off was crisp and not the knuckle-whitening experience of some flights, and Rebecca felt a surge of excitement as soon as the plane left the runway. It was too late to go back now, and she must look forward to her new life.

The drinks trolley came round and she ordered orange juice and mineral water, knowing that on a long flight she would be too thirsty to drink alcohol except with the meal offered. She poured out some water and drank it. It was cold and had a satisfying bite to it, and she drank it with the kind of satisfaction she had noticed when Sister Faith drank plain water. I shall look back on silly things like this, she thought, and the knowledge of what she would have to face suddenly shocked her.

Her tissue was wet and still the stupid tears coursed down her cheeks. What a fool I am! she thought. What a weak idiot! She kept her head bowed to hide her tears and sensed that someone was standing by her side, watching her. The shadow moved away, and when she looked up it was gone. A passenger on the way to the loo or a steward trying to get by with a tray, she thought, and found she felt better, as if the tears had washed away a lot of pain, a great deal of loneliness and most of her fear. She drank more water, then dozed until the meal trays were handed out for an early lunch.

'There's telly, Mum,' said the boy hopefully, having abandoned the view from the window.

'Later,' his mother said mechanically. 'Read your book and be quiet.'

Rebecca hired earphones and tuned in to light music, more to protect herself from the conversation beside her than for any love of old tunes. She closed her eyes and slept, and was awakened only when the next snack appeared and she treated herself to a tiny bottle of red wine.

The boy pushed past to go to the lavatory and then his mother went too, and Rebecca thought that if she followed they could all settle down again, so she made her way to the back of the plane. The seats were full and the air-conditioning was blowing hard through the small outlets over the seats, making a sound like the track on science fiction tapes. A man seated in the middle bent to get something under his seat, and Rebecca once more had the feeling that Anthony Brent was near. She stared, but he didn't come up while she was there, and the girl next to him looked familiar.

Back in her seat, she tried to recall the face of the girl. I must have seen her at the airport, she decided, but the face remained in her memory. The girl on the plane had short fair hair and was wearing a bright red dress. Her face was made up and her lips were scarlet to match the dress, but if she could change the dress for something white and simple, wipe away the make-up, she would be left with the girl in the photographs.

Her heart beat furiously. The aircraft was routed all the way to Khartoum, so what was she doing on this plane if Anthony Brent wasn't there?

'Sorry,' said Rebecca as she tried to go to the back of the plane again.

'Could you use the one at the front, madam? We're bringing the duty-free round now,' the stewardess said.

Rebecca sank back into her seat and ordered a bottle of brandy that would be useful medicinally even if she didn't want it to drink for social reasons, but she refused all the rest as she knew she couldn't carry it.

From time to time she glanced back, but could see nothing of the row in which the girl sat, and by the time the plane landed and the heat of Khartoum hit her, she believed she was imagining the resemblance.

The air-conditioned airport was a blessing that gave way to heat as she ventured out to find the taxi that Sister Faith said would take her to a hotel for the night, and she saw the cardboard notice with the name of the Mission on it and the name of the hotel. As she opened the door of the taxi, a man joined her, and two Sudanese who looked at her without smiling. The man, however, smiled and said, 'I'm Kurt Heiney, one of the medics on this trip. I saw you on the plane and wondered if you were joining us. Didn't you see the rest of the party? They had a spot of Customs mix-up, but they'll be with us later.'

Rebecca smiled with relief. Kurt looked solid and good-looking and intelligent. His blond hair was almost white from exposure to the sun and his face was tanned with much more than a few weeks on a sun-lounger.

'You've been here for a long time?' she asked.

'I thought I was working my way round the world, but I found the Sisters and got stuck,' he told her with a rueful grin. 'I took a couple of weeks off to see Egypt, and now I'm on my way back again.'

'When do you go back to America?'

'Next month or the month after. Or that's what I've been saying for the last six months.' He sighed. 'I know people will say there's as much deprivation in the US of A as there is here, but brother, they don't know the half of it!' he laughed. 'I mustn't put you off. It's good to see fresh faces, and we do have fun some of the time.'

The taxi stopped in front of a dusty entrance and Rebecca struggled out with her luggage that seemed caught up with a vast rug that one of the Sudanese carried. In the foyer, Kurt paused, and said with a certain formality, 'Sister Perivale, may I present Dr Gamel Bara, our expert on tropical diseases.'

The taller of the Sudanese bowed slightly but made no attempt to touch her hand. 'I am delighted to meet you, Sister,' he said, and his face changed as he smiled.

'You speak English very well,' Rebecca said impulsively.

'Scottish,' he said. 'I trained at Edinburgh and London, so I should speak your language even if I haven't absorbed all your beliefs and customs.' He swept his long white djellaba after him in a flowing train and picked up his hand luggage. The other man followed, carrying the rug and the other parcels.

'Who's the other man?' asked Rebecca. 'Doesn't he speak English?'

'That's Bara's servant, who goes everywhere with him and makes himself useful in a hundred ways as he knows the locals and can get news before we can. Quite harmless,' Kurt replied to Rebecca's unspoken question.

The huge overhead fans stirred the air but did little to cool the reception area, and already the fine cotton was damp on her back. Rebecca moved as slowly as possible when she was taken to her room and found to her relief that she had a shower to herself in one corner of the room. Not the Ritz, but sheer heaven, she thought as she revelled in the lukewarm water, then changed into fresh clothes.

'Ready for a meal?' called Kurt. 'It's cool in the restaurant. Come down as soon as you can and I'll buy you a drink.'

She applied a pale lipstick but no other make-up and piled her hair high on her head to keep her neck cool. The simple Swiss cotton shirt hung loose from her shoulders and the soft baggy trousers gave her a relaxed and comfortable air, the pastel colours muted and pleasing to eyes used to the glare of the sun. She strolled down, and Kurt looked at her with approval. 'You look cool as a lime,' he told her. 'Welcome to Khartoum.'

The restaurant and bar were cool and well furnished

and the drinks cold but not iced. 'We don't risk ice even in here,' said Kurt. 'Most of the time it's safe in a hotel like this, but if you never have it, you never forget, so when the water is contaminated, you don't suffer.'

'Lesson one,' said Rebecca, raising her glass.

'No, lesson two. You've already instinctively learned the first one.'

'What's that?' Rebecca wanted to know.

'In a Muslim country, women cover their arms and legs, and you look just right,' he said, and grinned. 'Even Bara can't keep the very grudging approval out of his eyes!'

They joined Dr Bara, who was sipping a glass full of dark red liquid. Rebecca looked at it, wondering if this was one custom he had taken back with him. If he was Muslim, how did he have a large glass of red wine to drink?

'You must try it,' said Dr Bara, smiling. 'Kirkady, to give it its shorter name. Non-alcoholic, very refreshing and easy to make.'

'What is it?' she asked.

'It's infused from dried hibiscus flowers, and you'll find it verra easily all over North Africa. It infuses like tea and then cools, and we add a lot of sugar, but that's a matter of taste, rather like you Sassenachs having sugar instead of salt with your porridge.'

Rebecca was enchanted. The soft Scottish burr coming from a face as dark as Africa was amazing. Kurt was laughing too, and when Dr Bara turned away he gave Rebecca the thumbs-up sign as if she had passed some kind of test.

Her heart warmed to these people, but she wanted to know more. 'How many are coming with us to the camp?' she asked.

'You, me, Bara and his servant, another doctor and an engineer who have been here before this trip, and a Sister from VSO seconded to us for the third time for short periods. We have some personnel at the camp, but this is the main changeover. I saw the other team while you were showering and they've checked in for a very long sleep before leaving for the UK.

'What do I call you?' he asked. 'We have Rebeccas at home, but they don't look like you.'

'Some people call me Becky,' she said. 'In training, when we used last names, I was called Perry. Take your choice.' It was the first time for ages that she had told any man he could call her Becky, but Kurt was so warm and comforting and brotherly that she hoped he would be a close friend.

'That's great,' he said. 'Becky it is. Hello, my new friend.'

'When do we meet the others, and when do we leave here?' asked Rebecca.

'We have to load up and get some more stores, but we're almost ready to go.' He looked serious. 'I hope you have some good shoes and strong pants for the ride. It's tough.'

'I came prepared,' she told him. 'Sister Faith told me what to pack, and she seemed to have lots of good ideas, even if she dresses in a habit all the time herself.'

'They wear thin ones at the camp,' said Kurt. 'And I think they're as cool as the djellabas the locals wear. Shall we eat?' he asked her.

'Should we wait for the others?' she asked. There was a nagging feeling that told her she must meet these people to see if they fitted in as well as Kurt and Dr Bara had done, and she couldn't lose the impression that the girl on the plane had been Meryl Sachs.

'You'll see enough of them during the next three months,' said Kurt. 'And it's a long time since I had a pretty girl all to myself for an evening.'

They ate chicken in a hot sauce and baked fish and *foule*, a mush of lentils, eaten with flat Arab bread, and Rebecca drank her first glass of Kirkady under the watchful eye of Dr Bara.

'It's good, but a bit too sweet for me,' she said, and the doctor ordered more with less sugar, which she enjoyed. 'I could drink a lot of this,' she said, and helped herself to more from the jug.

'I shall instruct Hamid to make it for you whenever possible,' said Dr Bara. 'It's better for you than alcohol in this climate.' She nodded. It made sense, and she knew she would be happy to drink soft drinks for the next three months.

Dr Bara frowned. He had searched inside his robes and obviously not found what he wanted.

'You can't chew betel here, Bara, unless you brought your own.'

'I forgot, so what am I to do?' Once more the Scottish voice made Rebecca smile, then she gasped.

'Wait here! I have something that you might like,' she said. She ran to her room and fetched a few packets of the chewing gum that Maeve had insisted she have and almost shyly offered them to the imposing man. He gave a deep chuckle and peeled off the paper.

'Welcome to Africa, Sister Becky,' he said.

Kurt was amused and teased Rebecca for having found out the doctor's vices before she left England, but she hotly denied the accusation. 'I hate to think what's in my dossier,' he said, 'and as for the others, what dark secrets have you unearthed about them?'

'I haven't met them,' she said.

'Any time now,' said Kurt lazily. 'Get that rig . . . when will she learn?' he groaned.

Rebecca turned and the glass of Kirkady nearly fell from her grasp. Meryl Sachs came towards them, dressed in a see-through blouse and tight skirt of bright green, and heavy junk ear-rings flashed on her hairline. Rebecca looked past her at the man who now bent to take her hand.

'Welcome to Africa,' said Anthony Brent.

CHAPTER FIVE

'HAMID will drive the truck and Kurt the Range Rover,' said Dr Bara firmly. 'The ladies can go by bus to Gedaref and take some of the equipment with them while we follow with the rest. After that, we shall be more cramped and hot, but at least we can spend a night in Gedaref and have showers.'

'Isn't Gedaref out of your way?' asked Rebecca. 'It goes east after we leave the Blue Nile, and the camp is a hundred miles from Gallabat, isn't it?'

'The road is very good to Gedaref and is routed that way to avoid sudden flooding of the Blue Nile,' Dr Bara explained. 'In the past that was a real danger, but we pray it will happen this year, because with the terrible drought in Ethiopia, everything fed by the Blue Nile has dried up, and river beds are now roads that could turn into fast-flowing torrents when the rains come.'

Anthony Brent remained silent. He had taken one look at Rebecca's suddenly pale and horrified face and done little more than make polite remarks to her when he could no longer avoid doing so, but the others had noticed nothing of the tension between them, putting down her gasp of surprise to a natural reaction to meeting someone she had thought was back in the UK.

'I thought we'd travel by truck,' said Rebecca. 'Sister Faith said she did.'

'Originally, people flew to Port Sudan and took the train to Gedaref, but now the train is so crowded with refugees that it's impossible to travel that way and bring

84

in supplies safely, so we use the Khartoum route.'

'A bus sounds very self-indulgent,' said Rebecca, smiling. 'I thought it would be far more difficult.'

'You speak too soon,' said Dr Bara. 'After Gedaref, the way is hard.'

'You'll crumple,' said Anthony Brent in a low voice. 'Go back home, Rebecca. This is no place for you.'

She looked up defiantly. 'If Sister Faith can stay out here, then I can for a short time.'

'You must see where the two Niles meet before we leave,' said Kurt. 'The others can finish loading and we have an hour to spare.' He took her where the two rivers met, one the Blue Nile from Ethiopia which comes from the mountains with such force after rain that it holds back the White Nile that comes from Uganda.

'It isn't very impressive,' said Rebecca, trying to read the battered notice that explained the source of each river. 'But I do believe the Blue Nile *is* bluer than the White.'

'I'll take a picture,' said Kurt. 'One for my collection.'

'Girls I've photographed by the Nile?' smiled Rebecca.

'Something like that,' he said, and grinned. 'I took a series of them of Meryl last trip and some of the two together.'

'Two?' queried Rebecca.

'Yeah. She wanted Tony in everything, but it was a busy time, and I wonder if she ever did make it with him.'

Already the sun beat down relentlessly and Rebecca was glad to drink her last glass of Kirkady and join Meryl on the air-conditioned coach. It was a delightful surprise to sit back on a reclining seat and be driven over good roads for mile after mile, even if the view was boring, being mainly yellow earth and sand, stunted trees and a few isolated huts.

Meryl offered her a cigarette, but Rebecca shook her head. 'No vices?' asked Meryl, after she had lit her own. 'Kirkady and long sleeves last night, and such a small pack so as not to overload the truck!'

'Sister Faith gave me a lot of advice,' said Rebecca calmly. 'And I'm much too lazy to carry too much in this heat.'

I must be nice to her, she thought. I've got to work with her for the next few months, and we shall be a close community.

The smoke made Meryl's eyes half close and she looked very thoughtful. 'When Tony said you'd be coming, I didn't picture you as you are.' She gave a malicious smile. 'He seemed very concerned, as if you might snap in the middle, but Sister Faith will try to get anyone, however unsuitable, so he couldn't object.'

'I came because I wanted to,' said Rebecca. 'I had no idea Mr Brent would be here and I'm sorry he is, as I doubt if we shall get on very well together.'

'Mr Brent? My, you haven't got far, have you? Tony and I have had some very good times together.' Meryl seemed satisfied that the new Sister would be no threat to her and became more friendly. 'He hates small women,' she said. 'It's nothing about you that he dislikes, but because out of a family of very healthy girls who do absolutely everything, the one tiny girl whom he adored died of polio, contracted in India. I've seen her picture and you remind me of her. He must see the likeness, so if he's a bit offhand, that will be the reason.'

Rebecca sat back and closed her eyes. It wasn't fair that Anthony Brent should judge everyone against his own flock of Brent geese! She smiled. That was what they were, a flock that must all conform to one image, and when someone didn't fit into that mould, he was uneasy and suspicious, unable to believe that they could be different, and successful.

In the distance they could see the Range Rover and big truck following the bus, keeping away from the dust thrown up on the road and looking far more hot than the roomy bus.

'How did you come to be here?' asked Rebecca, at last.

'I joined VSO for two years, to see the world, believe it or not. I didn't think it would be as bad, but I do love the work. It's just that I long for the bright lights at times, so I try to be seconded to smaller camps and have breaks in between, like this last one in London when they wanted someone to talk to a society collecting for refugees.' Meryl laughed. 'I can talk the hind leg off a donkey, so they send me, and it does give me some fun.'

'I'm here for three months or six, depending on how it goes,' said Rebecca.

'Or if you can stand it,' said Meryl. 'Even Bara has been known to go down with a dose of dysentery, and the new ones go down like flies,' she said, with relish.

'And you've never suffered in that way, I suppose?' asked Rebecca.

Meryl flushed. 'In the early days,' she admitted, 'and once when we all had it.' She stubbed out her cigarette. 'Not any more. I'm immune to most things—bugs, bad water and all other men but Tony.' She glanced sideways at Rebecca and once more she felt that Meryl was warning her that Anthony Brent was her property and let no girl fresh from London forget it.

'I did come to work,' said Rebecca. 'I left behind someone who wants to marry me and set up a smart health spa,' she added. 'I have to go back there some day and decide what to do.' If I seem frank with her, she thought, she may dismiss me as uninteresting and no challenge, and we could get on well as far as work is concerned. Meryl had told her of some of the common conditions she would find in the camp, and in spite of her unfortunate manner, she obviously loved the work and cared deeply what happened to the sick babies.

So it was with regret that the two girls climbed down from the coach and fetched their packs and two large cases from the trunk under the vehicle. The Range Rover was driving slowly into a parking bay and the truck followed.

Gedaref was hot and a film of dust hung in the air. Rebecca began to sense that this was the end of comfort, the end of cool drinks and the beginning of hardship. A drinks cooler stood under an awning, and she thankfully bought a large bottle of Coca-Cola. It was cold and although not her favourite soft drink, it was just what she needed. 'What now? Do we go on?' she asked, as it was late afternoon.

'We have a room for the night and we can shower,' said Kurt. He laughed. 'When I say a room, that's what I mean—one room for the lot of us, with simple mattresses and no privacy.'

'Surely there's somewhere else?' she asked, not fancying the idea of six people sharing.

'Hamid has looked, but this is a public holiday and every room is taken. You see, they come from miles around. This is the centre of civilisation for many Sudanese. That Coca-Cola stand is pure Western decadence, and they love it.' He laughed. 'Distances are so great here that towns as big as this are few and they attract many people. Look!' he said.

Rebecca stared at the long line of camels and donkeys moving through the town. 'There must be two hundred or more!' she exclaimed. The camel rugs glowed with every bright colour possible to weave into fabric, and the men were tall and fierce-looking, with voluminous robes of pure white.

'They're nomadic and will stay only for supplies and water and be gone by morning,' said Kurt. He took a swig of his drink, then yawned. 'We must rest,' he said. 'Tomorrow, like the Arabs, we fold our tents and go before the sun is up.'

'I feel as if I've been tossed back into the Old Testament,' said Rebecca as Meryl walked with her to the shower room. The equipment was spartan but gave out gushes of cold water that refreshed her.

'Don't dry your top half,' called Meryl. 'Soak a tee-shirt in water to wear in bed. It's the only way to keep cool, and you can't get chilled in this heat.'

Rebecca dried carefully and put on a thin shirt of soft pink Sea Island cotton worn loose outside her trousers. There would be no means of undressing and lying in night clothes, and this was practical and as cool as she could imagine being in Gedaret.

'You look . . . fresh,' said Anthony Brent. He stood aside to let her walk back to the room and followed her, his hair wet and his damp towel round his neck to keep cool. 'We're eating at the hotel over there,' he told her. 'Bara and Hamid have gone to friends and will be here at five in the morning, so we eat and sleep and be ready for the off.' He rubbed a trickle of water from his face and looked at her in such a way that she felt like a small child who had done something not bad, but inconvenient. 'You shouldn't have come,' he told her, 'but now you are here, can we start again?'

'I hope we can work together,' she said. 'And I shall need advice, as I'm new to this.' If that could be their relationship, she could bear the bad times when she yearned for his touch, longed for his kiss, and treasured the crumbs of attention he could spare from Meryl, she thought. At least she must try, as that was all she could expect.

'Take care, Rebecca,' Anthony cautioned. 'Avoid drinking the water, and be sure to come for pills as soon as you feel under the weather. Don't put off telling someone if you feel ill.' He smiled. 'I didn't say I was coming here as I suspected you wouldn't be seen with me anywhere, let alone in such restricted conditions, but I had no right to stop you.'

'I don't hate you,' she began.

'I didn't think you did, but you haven't exactly given me a come-on. Paul Weldon means more to you than I thought, and he'll be waiting when you return.'

'Maybe,' shrugged Rebecca. 'But meanwhile, Mr Brent, I'd rather forget England and deal with whatever I have to do here.'

'It would be better if you called me Tony,' he said. 'Everyone does, and I already call you Rebecca, or hadn't you noticed?' He sounded wistful, but she couldn't say call me Becky. It stuck somewhere in her throat and in her heart. Friends used that name, family did too, and it had irritated her when Paul used it. Somewhere along the line in the past, it had become a privilege that she didn't give to everyone. She couldn't bear to hear it spoken in that deep musical voice unless it was important to him as much as it would be to her.

'Fine, Tony,' she said, and smiled.

'Ready?' called Kurt. He wore a singlet soaked in

water and his pale hair was like a pad of cotton wool drying slowly.

'Doesn't anyone have a towel here?' asked Rebecca, laughing.

'You have,' said Kurt. 'I was rather looking forward to seeing you win Miss Wet Tee-shirt of Sudan this year!' His gaze roamed over her shirt and the hidden curves, and Rebecca began to think his interest wasn't altogether brotherly.

Meryl came out of the shower unit and hung her towel on a hook on the wall. 'That will dry in an hour,' she said, then laughed. 'Did Dr Bara chicken out again?' she asked. Her tee-shirt was tight and soaking wet and she wore no bra. She looked at Tony with blatant defiance edged with desire, and he seemed not to notice that her nipples pointed aggressively through the fabric.

'Gee, you have the nicest Montgomery Tubercles this side of the Atlantic,' said Kurt. 'I've seen boobs, but you show more, and the natives will go wild!' He was laughing, and suddenly Meryl went red and snatched up a bra and disappeared into the lavatory.

'Sorry about that,' said Kurt, 'but she should know better. Meryl is a great girl, but this is Africa and the Sudan, where women are different.'

'Is that why Dr Bara isn't eating with us?' asked Rebecca.

'Partly,' said Kurt. 'Meryl gets up his nose a bit. Not that I object,' he added, with a knowing look. 'She should behave in public, but we all need something to do during the long hot nights.'

Rebecca looked away, and saw Tony Brent watching her. He was smiling, and a kind of bond formed between them for a moment. He rubbed his hair more vigorously and hung his towel up too, then carefully combed his hair and did up two buttons on his shirt. 'You can wait for Meryl, Kurt. She'll need flattering after you put her down, and that's your job. Rebecca and I are the only civilised ones here, so see you at table.' He tucked her hand under his arm and drew Rebecca away. 'Hungry?' he asked.

His hand was cool after the shower and his damp body was hard against her side as they walked down to the restaurant. A slick of wet hair fell over his face and she wanted to comb it back, press waves into the darkness and find out if he had a bump of domesticity under the thatch at the base of his skull, an erotic zone best avoided when kissing, she thought, and her hands itched to take his head down to her level to have his kiss.

Maybe the heat will cool my feelings, she thought dismally. No man could see Meryl as she was and not desire her, and if he really cared, then he had to leave her to Kurt, looking like that, or they would never have joined the others for food! The wet tee-shirt was much more suggestive than going topless. So I'm like his little sister, which made him doubt my strength and ability, Rebecca thought, but now will be useful as he can use me to act as a kind of buffer between them when his emotions get too much to bear!

He had said, 'One day you'll look round and find me there,' but not like this, she wanted to say. I want you to look *at* me, to see me as a woman in love, not as a memory of a little sister, a relic of a memory of your mother and a butterfly brooch.

'Can you bear more *foule*?' he asked. 'It's a staple food here and isn't as foul as it's pronounced. Eat freshly cooked fish and meat and vegetables—and avoid the watercress.'

'Why that? It looks green and fresh.'

'Dracontiasis, or Guinea Worm, is spread through a tiny shellfish called Cyclops which contaminates water. This cress might be grown in bad water or washed in it, and is to be avoided.'

'Sister Faith mentioned Guinea Worm,' said Rebecca.

'They say it's the fiery serpent that attacked the Children of Israel when they were on the shores of the Red Sea, and it takes time to be felt. The worm erupts under the skin after anything up to two years and gives a high temperature and local swelling.'

'How do we cope with it?' she asked.

'By cutting the skin and pulling out the worm,' he said calmly. 'Almost as they did in the Old Testament, and of course we can control it with Thiabendazole and Niridazole now, which cures them in no time, but the ones that have already formed have to be extracted.' He grinned. 'You shall have first crack at the next bunch —one of the exciting things you do if you insist on coming here!'

'Thank you very much,' she said. 'No salads, no watercress.'

Kurt waved from the doorway and Meryl followed him, looking slightly chastened, but respectably dressed. The sluggish fans over the tables did little to cool the air and the noise of camels objecting to everything, combined with the smell of donkeys, did little to make the meal memorable. No one said a lot, and they retired to their room to lie on the beds and stare at the ceiling. Half an hour later, Dr Bara and Hamid joined them and they all lay still, no one sleeping much, and Rebecca at least wondering how she could bear three months of being thought of as a pretty little sister who must be protected for her own sake.

At four, a camel snarled loudly under the window and the caravan moved off. Kurt ordered bread and jam, and lemon juice mixed with lime and diluted with bottled water, and by five the truck was covered with canvas, the Range Rover stacked high with packages, and somewhere among the clutter were four people, Kurt driving, Meryl and Rebecca sitting precariously at the back and Tony Brent on a box in the passenger seat beside Kurt.

The sun was a rim of dull anger over the desert as it rose and tinted the hills. Camels walked along the skyline, driven by men in white robes and others with coloured headdresses and embroidered saddles. Water in the carrier under Rebecca's feet slurped and gurgled, and the bottles of soft drinks she had brought on the vehicle took up more room than she had anticipated.

Kurt had said that a town called Doka would be sighted after fifty miles, but the road was the roughest and most uneven fifty miles that Rebecca had ever endured. Her elbows were sore as she tried to brace herself against the sides of the hot car and her throat was dry from the dust that seemed to seep into everything, but she was determined that she would not be the one to ask for a stop for water and a rest.

Hamid was driving the truck, and his white turban showed clearly as the two Sudanese made good progress and seemed unaffected by the heat. The truck put on speed and the Range Rover followed to a group of small mud huts that Tony said was Doka. It was nothing like the town that Rebecca expected, but she climbed thankfully down to ease her aching limbs.

Hamid was crouching over a small fire over which a black pot was steaming. He threw in a handful of tea and as they sat in the shade of the one-roomed hospital, they all drank hot sweet *chai* and found it refreshing, but as usual with drinks in the Sudan, very sweet.

'What now?' asked Rebecca. Her skirt stuck to her back and her hands were clammy with the heat.

'We go on towards Gallabat, then turn off halfway to the camp, but I thought you'd want a break here,' said Dr Bara. His white smile was comforting and Rebecca was glad she had done nothing to offend him.

'No more towns like Gedaref?' she asked. Already that dusty, inadequate place seemed like luxury. She gazed out across the scrubland and up at the ball of fire that was the sun.

'No more towns,' said Dr Bara gravely, 'but there's Gallabat on the border where we can have hospital facilities if the need arises, and that's only thirty miles from the camp.'

'It's packed with refugees,' said Kurt. 'We're better using our own primitive facilities and we shall have enough to do just helping people to survive.' He tossed away the tea-leaves in his mug. 'That's why I stay in this goddam country,' he growled. 'How can I leave when they need so much?'

'You'll have to go back some day,' said Meryl. She looked at him with a question in her eyes. 'I thought of seeing America after I finish VSO.'

'I'll give you a few addresses,' he said, and she looked disappointed.

'In three months' time when we go back to hand over to the next team, we may feel we've had enough,' said Tony Brent. 'At least, some of us will want to get back to the comfort of the UK.'

'We'll have to wait and see,' said Rebecca. 'I may stay for six months, and take a break after three as Kurt did and see Egypt and the Pyramids.'

'You'll need a guide,' said Kurt, and Meryl tightened

her lips. Rebecca smiled and said nothing, but she knew Meryl would hate it if she got too friendly with either of the good-looking men who would have no other female company from a European background other than her and Rebecca for the next few months.

'When does Sister Faith get there?' asked Tony.

'I believe she's there now,' said Dr Bara. 'She cut short her convalescence and came last week, so you will have at least one friend to greet you, Rebecca.'

His smile was warm and gave her the feeling that he wanted to protect her, but it made Rebecca feel that he too thought of her as a small girl who needed help over every gate she came to and couldn't keep up with the big girls. I'm not all that small! she thought indignantly, and as yet I haven't grumbled at the heat or asked anyone to carry my pack.

She climbed into the Range Rover again and settled down on the hard boxes strapped to the seats. The rough edge of a wooden tea-chest dug into the soft flesh behind her knees and added to the discomfort, but she stuffed her light headscarf under her knees and hoped she wouldn't be raw when they got to the camp. The linen hat proved to be a good idea and Meryl looked far more overheated than she did, as she had only a scarf with her to protect her head.

Once more the drive seemed endless, and now groups of weary Ethiopians trudged along, carrying huge bundles, trying to reach Doka and then another camp further along the road to Gedaref. Babies clung to mothers, and young children walked like thin automata beside them.

'They'll never make it,' muttered Kurt, and drove to the truck.

'They're used to heat and deprivation and can go for a

Dear Susan,

Your special introductory offer of 4 free books is too good to miss. I understand they are mine to keep when the free clock subscription for me. If I decide to subscribe, I shall receive four brand new Masquerade romances every other month for just £6.00, post and packing free. If I decide not to subscribe, I shall write to you within 10 days. The free books are mine to keep in any case.

I understand that I may cancel or suspend my subscription at any time by writing to you. I am over 18 years of age.

4A8M

Name _____
(BLOCK CAPITALS PLEASE)
Address _____
_____
_____ Signature _____
_____ Postcode _____

To Susan Welland
Reader Service
FREEPOST
P.O. Box 236
CROYDON
Surrey CR9 9EL

NO
STAMP
NEEDED

SEND NO MONEY NOW

long time yet,' said Dr Bara evenly. 'At least they had water and food at the camp and may have heard of a food distribution by one of the charities along this road.' He turned to Rebecca. 'You must learn who can be helped and who must be left to die,' he told her. 'It's hard, but it is the will of Allah who is taken, and we must never waste our resources.'

Rebecca looked from one face to another and they all were solemn. Nobody contradicted the Sudanese doctor, and Rebecca hoped with all her heart that she would never have to make that decision.

The evening brought a slight relief from the heat and the sand stopped throwing up a furnace as they passed. A light breeze, hot but enough to stir the air, was a welcome change, and suddenly Hamid shouted something and waved.

Lights from a flaring kerosene lamp and a fire told them that this was the camp, and in a minute the vehicles were surrounded by shouting children and more reticent men and women, dressed in a mixture of Ethiopian and Western clothes.

A group of tidy mud huts with thatched roofs stood in a circle and showed the original settlement. Some had brick walls and a generator supplied electricity to a few of the buildings, but others were ramshackle and hastily repaired, and had no lights. Tents and shanties were pitched as far as the eye could see, and figures moved round tiny fires that looked like glow-worms in the dusk.

'I had no idea there'd be so many,' said Rebecca. 'How do they find food, and fuel for fires? We passed few trees and only scrub and cactus.'

'Some have camels and use the dried dung, and others cut down the cactus which makes a good fuel, but most have brought what wood they pick up on the way or what dried plants they can find. A kerosene stove is a luxury that's closely guarded, and we have to make sure that any supplies are shared out fairly when a truck arrives,' said Tony. He put up a hand to help her down, but Rebecca slid down out of reach. She pulled down her pack and asked where she could leave it, then a white-robed figure came along the dirt track and held out her arms.

'Sister Faith!' Rebecca ran towards her and hugged her. 'You look wonderful,' she smiled.

'God is good and I am among my people again,' said Sister Faith. 'Come with me and I'll show you your quarters.'

'Same hut, Sister?' asked Kurt, and hauled his pack over to catch up with Tony and Dr Bara. They disappeared into a brick-built hut with electricity, and Rebecca and Meryl were shown a smaller hut of similar construction with two beds, a desk and washstand and two chests for their possessions each with a key. Behind a curtain was a chemical toilet and the floor was beaten earth.

'Glad you came?' asked Meryl with more than a trace of sarcasm, as she began to unpack her things.

'It's wonderful to see Sister Faith,' said Rebecca, hoping her first culture shock wasn't showing.

'I'll show you round as soon as we've locked away all our things,' said Meryl. 'There's not much theft here as most of them respect the nuns, and if Hamid is here, he helps police the camp, but with so many travelling, and having so little, the odd bad apple slips in at times.'

Meryl had changed from the girl who seemed intent on being amoral to an efficient nursing Sister and Rebecca, as the next hour wore on, began to respect her. They saw the small hospital with its two couches used for

examinations and operations, the lamps fuelled by
kerosene and the ones that could go on precious electricity in an emergency, and the cupboards of drugs, dressings and instruments, all locked and with enough keys
for each member of the team to have copies.

There was a strange peace about the camp as the day
ended and the small fires cooked mealies and *foule* and
whatever rations had been given out. 'We eat after dark
and hope we finish for the night,' said Meryl. 'Today
Sister said there was a small group who stopped only for
a meal and some water. They were the ones we saw, but
tomorrow there may be crowds, so we get what rest we
can and cope.'

The well was situated at the end of the camp and a
rough bench and table and zinc bath were close by to
serve as a wash-house, where clothes could be washed,
but with the acute water shortage, no baths were permit-
ted. 'We carry our own buckets of water to wash in the
hut,' said Meryl, and from time to time she looked at
Rebecca, curiously, as if seeking some weakness or
abhorrence.

'Why do we have the best huts and extra water?' asked
Rebecca, when Meryl had poured out mugs of water
from a huge jar in the hut, boiled and left to cool. 'The
Sudanese helpers have mud and no lights and only rugs
as beds on the floor. I peeped in one,' she added.

'It all comes down to the fact that we're the ones who
can save lives,' said Meryl calmly. 'If we're ill, dozens
could die, because we haven't the people with skills to
take over from us. You must eat well, even if there are
hungry mouths all round you. You must rest when you
can and use water to keep scrupulously clean, even if
there's a shortage. People at home see pictures of plump
and healthy workers and ask why that's so when they're

surrounded by starvation, and when I give talks, I have to explain that my food would help one person but my skills can help hundreds.

'Now, I'll go and see if we can eat soon. I want to catch up on the news with one of the Sisters in Faith's lot who was here when I was the last time. I'll call when we're ready.'

Meryl slipped away and hurried over to the hospital, and Rebecca pushed the last of her clothes into the chest and locked it. The back of her knee was painful and she tried to look at it under the lamp. It was red and dusty, so she took a little water and washed the place carefully, but she knew a splinter from the packing case on which she had sat had gone through her jeans and into the skin.

'Anyone in?' called a voice. 'It's Tony.'

'Come in,' she said, then blushed, as her jeans lay on the bed and she was standing in her briefs under the lamp.

'Something wrong?' he asked, seeing the small bowl of water and the sponge.

'I've got a splinter in my leg,' she told him. 'I was going to find my tweezers, but I doubt if I can reach it. Meryl will be back soon and she can do it.'

'Lie on the bed on your front,' he commanded. From his pocket he produced a small case in which he had scissors, tweezers and a small scalpel in tubes of spirit. He dabbed the sore place with spirit and Rebecca nearly jumped off the bed. 'Lie still. If you can't stand a spot of spirit on you, you shouldn't have come,' he said calmly.

'You might have given me warning!' she protested.

'Do you always want warning before anything happens to you?'

'If it's going to hurt, yes! *Ouch!*'

'All out, but you were wise to see to it at once. In this

heat, small cuts and scrapes can be septic in a day. More spirit and a tiny plaster and you'll do,' he said.

He sat on the bed, and Rebecca wished she could grab her trousers, but he was sitting on one of the legs, and she couldn't remain on her tummy for ever. His hand touched her hair and then her neck, tracing the line of her spine until she wanted to scream. If I turn now, I shall be in his arms, she thought, and her sensation of being suffocated was only partly because she buried her head in the pillow.

'Time for dinner,' said Tony, and his voice was harsh as if he had difficulty in speaking. He turned her on to her back, and his mouth descended, cutting out the light, bringing another burst of light through her brain. Splinters of pain that were not in the flesh were agony, stabbing her with the knowledge that he wanted her, found her desirable, and yet was not for her. She returned his kiss in a desperate abandon, then struggled free. 'Meryl,' she gasped, reminding herself that he was Meryl's man.

'Meryl?' He shook his head to rid his mind of this fantasy, of a girl on a bed in an African hut who was warm and human and who returned his kisses as if starved, and he stood away. 'Yes, she'll be back soon,' he said. 'I'll wait for you outside.' He laughed without humour. 'I was right—you shouldn't have come here.'

'You didn't try to stop me,' she reminded him. 'You only taunted me with being inadequate, and I had no idea you'd be here.'

'Sister Faith made me promise not to tell you. She wanted you here, but for once the dear woman is wrong.'

Rebecca reached for her jeans and dressed hurriedly. Outside, the air was cooler and the sky bright with stars, and in the distance came the coughing roar of the wild.

She shivered. This was Africa, primitive and unpredictable. She walked beside Tony, but they were miles apart. His face was stern and he didn't look at her again until they reached the long table at which all the medical staff and the nuns sat for supper. I've shown that I love him, she thought, then she heard what Meryl was saying. She was talking to one of the nuns whom Rebecca had not met.

'Yes, Rebecca Perivale from Beattie's. This is her first time out.' Meryl laughed and her voice could be heard the length of the table, making sure that Kurt and Tony both heard what she was saying. 'It'll be the last time too. Her fiancé is starting a health farm in the UK and she'll be going back to that.'

'I haven't decided yet,' said Rebecca weakly. 'We aren't engaged.'

'But he has asked you,' said Meryl in the tone that indicated that they had been having girl-chats on the journey down and, yes . . . maybe she was giving away a confidence, but they were all friends, and it was such nice news.

Kurt raised an eyebrow and began to eat his food. Tony stared at her as if she had told a lie, and Sister Faith briskly told Kurt that they hadn't as yet said Grace, and he could wait for another minute before eating.

CHAPTER SIX

'TIME to get up,' said Meryl. She was wearing a cotton dress with short sleeves and a matching belt. She wore no make-up and her feet were in closed-in shoes that were comfortable rather than glamorous.

Rebecca struggled back to consciousness and sat on her bed. 'Surely not,' she muttered. 'It's the middle of the night!'

'Four a.m.,' said Meryl briskly, and Rebecca sensed her pleasure in telling her this unwelcome news. 'We have a truck arriving with a load of sick children and there'll be a procession of patients all day today for inoculations, food and treatment. I've left you some washing water. Just tip it outside over the pot of tomatoes. It's all the watering they get, but we do quite well for herbs and things that way. Breakfast is ready.'

She left Rebecca to sort out her thoughts, and dress in one of her thin cotton dresses, and shoes similar to those that Meryl had, that she had worn on duty when training to be a midwife.

Her knee no longer hurt, and she wondered if Tony had slept as well as she had for a few hours.

Meryl had been kind this morning, she thought. She could have made her fetch her own water, and she had left her alone to dress in peace. Perhaps she was sorry she had said too much at supper, but Rebecca knew she was once more warning her that Anthony Brent belonged to one woman.

With a deftness born of practice, she coiled her long

hair into a tight knot and pinned it to the top of her head. In a way it would act as a sun-hat, and perhaps she would have no need of her shapeless linen hat, but she took it with her to breakfast.

Kurt was eating fast. He broke a piece of flat bread and plastered it with vegetable extract, washing it down with weak coffee. 'This is good,' he said. 'You need the extra salt here, and this is full of it. Bad for me when I'm at home, they tell me, but here it's one thing I can have with a clear conscience.' He grinned. 'See you in fifteen minutes at the hospital. Eat up, you may miss lunch.'

Rebecca ate what she could, but a mixture of excitement and dread nearly closed her throat, but she drank two cups of coffee and ate a little bread. Meryl had gone and there was no way of putting off the unknown trials of the day, and when she went round to the entrance of the hospital she saw why everyone was hurrying.

In the light of a lamp, a queue of dark-skinned people lined up, waiting with a patience that was fatalistic and had an air of hopelessness. Most of them carried babies and some had bowls ready for food. A child with a pot-belly broke the line and peered up through the near darkness to Sister Faith, who was taking the children one by one and measuring their upper arms.

Rebecca stared. It seemed such a useless activity when there were dozens waiting to be fed. A red elastic band was put round the wrist of a small girl and a blue one on the wrist of a thin baby. The mother of the baby joined the line into the hospital bay, but was given a helping of sticky porridge, and a pint of water into her own water-bottle.

'Why the division? Surely they're all hungry?' queried Rebecca.

'They will have food,' said Sister Faith in a reassuring

voice, 'but those with red bands need extra nourishment as they're too thin for their body weight and we hope to save them. The others need inoculations against measles, because the side effects of chest infection and dehydration if they catch the disease can kill them in this weak state.'

'But why measure them? They're all in need.'

'You see that baby? The mother has brought her here without water for days. She won't give the baby water because she thinks diarrhoea is nature's way of cleansing the body, and the child is dying. There's nothing we can do for her, and we must care for those with a chance to live.'

'What about a drip? Even an old-fashioned sub-cutaneous infusion of saline?' Rebecca regarded Sister Faith with anxiety mixed with horror. Surely she couldn't be so hardhearted?

Sister Faith looked at her tenderly. 'Go inside and begin the feeds,' she said. 'You'll see what I mean. Today Kurt is putting up drips and subcuts and Meryl is mixing the anti-dehydration fluids which you and she will give to as many as will take it. You waste no time on the dying except to give them water if they can take it. There are thirty babies waiting for you, Sister Becky.' She called her back. 'Tell Anthony we have the vaccines he wanted and a supply of metal and glass syringes which will need sterilising.'

'No disposables?'

Sister Faith shook her head. 'We make do and we do well,' she said simply.

There were babies on every mattress, with a mother sitting on the ground beside the bed, and as Rebecca went from one to the next, the pattern emerged. If the child could take fluids by mouth a solution of glucose and saline was handed to the mother to feed the child, and this was made up by Meryl, using a two-ended plastic spoon, the smaller one filled with salt and the bigger end with glucose, which she mixed with a pint of sterile water. It looked primitive but gave a very good copy of the natural body fluids, and it could be prepared without much cost.

The more dehydrated were given solutions made up from proprietary brands of dehydration mixtures, including glucose, magnesium chloride and sodium chloride with amino-acids to help the lack of protein.

Within the next two hours Rebecca had introduced four nasal tubes into stomachs that craved fluid and left the mother in each case to hold the bottle that filled the tube gently and continuously. Most of the women co-operated and sat patiently until all the fluid was gone, rocking the children to sleep.

Other children she had almost force-fed until they got the taste for the strange liquids, and some could have thin gruel with added vitamins. To see the few who walked about gnawing huge slabs of flat bread covered with jam or vegetable extract was heartening, and once the children were filled with fluid, they often managed to eat, walk about and, sometimes, even to play.

Crying babies and the keening of women whose babies had died mixed with the moans of camels and donkeys and the dull thud of farm implements as the men dug graves for the dead, but inside the hospital and the huts surrounding it, the workers didn't hear this as they went from one to another tirelessly.

Rebecca looked up from the baby she held in her arms. Hamid looked down at her. 'You finish that one and come,' he instructed. Rebecca looked down the line of never-ending black faces. 'You come!' Hamid said firmly. 'My master says.' She gave the child back to his mother and smiled. He was drinking well now after five minutes' struggle and the woman could do the rest.

The heat struck her as she left the room and her knees felt weak, but she hurried into the long hut that served as dining room, common room and rest room for the staff. If Dr Bara needed her, it might be for inoculations. Rebecca washed her hands at the basin by the door and flapped her hands to dry them, recalling that one child had looked more ill than dehydrated and she might carry infection.

'Sister Becky,' said Dr Bara, 'sit down and drink this.'

'I thought you needed me,' she said, and took the pint mug of *lemoon*, the lime and lemon drink she had tasted in Gadaref.

'I do. I need you today, tomorrow and for a long time, but if you lose fluid, you'll be of no use,' he said sternly. 'The others have been in, but I suppose they forgot to tell you.' She drained the mug and only then knew just how hot and tired she was. There was a slightly salty taste to the *lemoon* under the sweetness. She smiled, and Dr Bara laughed. 'You like my own brand of rehydration? I think I must take out a patent for it.'

'Couldn't the children have it?' she asked. 'It tastes better than the solutions we give.'

'There isn't enough,' he said. 'Now what did you have this morning?'

'Bread and coffee,' she told him.

'Very little, I suspect. Your first morning, and the strangeness made you lose your appetite.' She laughed. If I close my eyes, she thought, he could be a comfortable and chiding Scottish doctor, and yet when I look at him, he's this tall, rather frightening-looking Sudanese.

'Very little,' she admitted.

'Eat these now,' he ordered, 'and take ten minutes' break.' He handed her a saucer full of fresh dates. 'Hamid washed them well in pure water, so they're safe to eat,' he said. At the entrance, he swung round, his djellaba eddying and adding to the impression he made. 'You eat every one, and you do *not* give them to the children!'

Rebecca ate and felt decidedly better. She went out into the heat and across the flat bare earth to the hospital again. Meryl was taking down a subcutaneous infusion and the woman holding the baby was weeping. 'Too late,' said Meryl in a flat voice. 'It still gets me.'

'Do we boil these here?' asked Rebecca.

'You're catching on. It's our only means of sterilising, apart from soaking in disinfectant. There are several sets waiting to be cleaned and boiled. Run them through with clean water and do as many as you can together to save fuel and water, then leave them covered, in the water. We use them soon enough to make that possible, and if we have some over, Sister Faith puts them under sheets soaked in carbolic.' Meryl smiled wryly. 'I was always scathing about the things they had to do during the last war. Our Tutor told us about wet sets used in theatre, but I must confess that I now have the greatest respect for them, coping with a continuous stream of cases with so few amenities, and after being here I know I can do anything, anywhere.'

'You're very efficient,' Rebecca told her.

'Yes, I am, and I do care about these people.' Meryl looked almost apologetic. 'It gets me so much that I have to have fun now and again, or I'd go mad.' She glanced at Rebecca. 'Can you cope now? The last lot have been inoculated and the women have got the message about feeding, and some are leaving for Gedaref as soon as it gets cooler.'

'Are you leaving?' asked Rebecca.

'Kurt has to take two cases to Gallabat today. It's stupid—they both came through the town yesterday and could have stayed for operations then. I hope we get there before they have burst appendices.'

'Can't we do them?'

'We could, but not now, with all these people coming continuously. Surgery, unless it's a local kind, has to be transferred. We have no helicopter and no real ambulance except for a truck that someone adapted with an awning and fixed beds.'

'So you're going too?' said Rebecca.

'Yes, we'll help if necessary and pick up a few bits of equipment off the train. Someone has to go, and they say there'll be no more refugees tonight as the police in Gallabat have stopped issuing visas for two days. That's another reason for going. If they're flooded with people who can't come here, Kurt and I can cope for a while with the hospital.'

'Is there a hotel?'

'Not for us. Full of flea-ridden people, and we have the ambulance. Quite comfortable if we can find shade to park.' Meryl gave Rebecca a look that challenged her to believe she would sleep with Kurt, then turned away.

Hamid called the helpers to lunch and they sat round the table eating *foule* and dried fish made into a kind of stew. *Lemoon* and Kirkady were available, and when Rebecca refused Coca-Cola, Dr Bara laughed. 'It's good for you. I wouldn't say that in Europe, but here it probably supplies many of the mineral salts you need.' Conversation was exclusively about the work, and Sister

Faith organised everyone in such a way that they knew exactly what to do and no one felt any resentment that they were working harder than the rest.

'Finish the sterilising and put out a wet set,' said Sister Faith, 'then rest on your bed for an hour as the heat will try you. Meryl and Kurt have gone, taking food with them for the journey and the night so that they eat nothing there. I think the visas have been stopped as news of another cholera outbreak came from across the Ethiopian border, so they've promised to be self-sufficient.

'Anthony, will you tell Rebecca more about the work and let her put up a drip, as with all those eager little house surgeons at Beattie's, she may not have had a lot of practice.'

Everyone knew what to do, and Hamid came and went, busy all day with drinks and food, and then had time to explain treatments to many of the refugees who spoke no English. Rebecca's admiration for the whole staff grew and she gladly did everything she was told to do.

'I've never put up an intravenous,' she confessed. 'Sister Faith is right—there are many areas that have been taken over by doctors, things that in the last war nurses did as there was no other qualified staff to cope, but gradually we've been shouldered out, and even in midwifery we have less influence.'

'You're doing very well,' said Tony. 'Found the vein the first time in, and it *is* a bit collapsed. Now strap it well, as they get restless and the mother will be too frightened to touch it.'

'You gave me confidence,' she said. 'But then you all seem so practical and dedicated that it's easy to follow.'

'Bara will be on my tail if I keep you here. If Sister

Faith gives an order, he sees that it's carried out, and if you don't toe her line, heaven help you! She said rest and so you must.' He looked at her with a kind of wonder. 'You don't seem tired.'

'I'm too stimulated by all this,' she explained. 'But if I lie down, I know I shall go to sleep and forget the time. I didn't bring an alarm that works. Meryl has one, but she took it with her.'

'I'll wake you with a drink and tell you what needs doing.' Rebecca watched Tony take the soiled swabs to the small bonfire kept for destroying all infected and dirty material. In a huge modern hospital, he would never do that. She smiled. He was brown in the sun and his hands were freckled on the backs where the sun highlighted the soft hairs on the backs of his hands. His hair was tousled after bending over a dozen babies and holding those who didn't really see the need for sharp needles in their buttocks, and her heart did odd and tender things. Beautiful men were rare, and his beauty came from strength and health and intelligence, with a slumbering passion that geared his work, his movements and . . . his deeper emotions.

Meryl had gone, once more with the predatory gleam in her eyes that she had had in the town, and Kurt had looked at her as if he approved. I could be like her, Rebecca thought. All the hard work, the heat and the throb of something primeval that was Africa made her want to fling off her clothes and lie naked on her bed, but she didn't feel safe if Tony Brent was coming to waken her. She took off her belt and shoes and lay on the bed with the soft cotton dress clinging to her. The mug of water by her side was already warm, and she made a face as she sipped it, as it was well-water, and even boiled, it still tasted brackish.

Outside, a group of women were making bread, flattening it in their hands and cooking it on heated flat stones over a smoky fire, and they crooned softly as they worked, with one voice taking up the words, singing and fading, and Rebecca heard it die away in her sleep.

It was a deep pit into which she slipped and rested. Weariness caught up with her and she gave in to it completely, like a child or a pet that falls asleep where it is playing. Her hair lay across the pillow in a waving veil of brightness, as she had unpinned it to leave her head free of the tight knot that made rest impossible, and when Tony came in, after tapping softly on the door, carrying a cup of hot *chai* and biscuits, she was still sound asleep, her hand under her cheek and her rosy lips innocent and sweet.

'Michelle!' he exclaimed, with an involuntary start, and put the cup down on the table. He came to the bedside and touched the bright hair, picking up a strand and taking it to his lips. He looked down at the girl on the bed and watched the gentle lift and fall of her breast and the pulse that beat evenly in her throat.

Rebecca stirred and her eyelids fluttered. She moved her head away from his hand and opened her eyes.

'Tony!' she said, and held out her arms, still bemused with sleep. It seemed right for him to be there, with the strong hands caressing her hair. It was right that he should bend over her with such a look of love in his eyes that she had to hold him close, but she saw his expression change, become guarded and bitter. He pressed his lips to her cheek and then found her mouth, eagerly seeking her response, and his hands found her soft breasts and lingered over her fast beating heart.

He kissed her as if to wipe out a bad memory and to convince himself that she was alive and human and

Rebecca felt he wanted her very much—but something was wrong.

The sweetness of her awakening came back to her. 'Who's Michelle?' she asked at last, when he sat on the edge of the bed, gazing down at her, perplexed.

'Does it matter?' he asked in a low voice.

'Yes, it matters,' she said simply. 'I look like her, don't I?'

Tony nodded. 'You're two people, Rebecca. It's like seeing the past and yet knowing that you had no part in it. It's like trying to see you as my dead sister and then knowing that I'm certainly not your brother!' He sat away from her and handed her the cup. His voice was husky. 'When you sit there with all that wonderful hair over your face, holding the cup in both hands and looking at me over the top of it, you're like Michelle, but when I hold you in my arms, you're a woman I desire above any other creature.'

'And both illusions fade as soon as we're with other people,' she said sadly. 'Men find me attractive, so why not you?' Her voice was defiant to hide her sadness.

'You're beautiful,' he told her. 'Any man with red blood in his veins would want you, but I know you're not for me. Meryl told me of your plans, and I suppose you're wise to settle down with Paul Weldon. You're much too fragile to stay here or to endanger your health by overworking.'

'I'm not fragile!' Rebecca protested. 'Just because I'm not as big as your hockey-playing sisters it doesn't mean I'm about to snap in two!' She glared at him and slid off the bed to find her hairbrush.

'Michelle was so much like you,' he said, as if wanting her to understand.

'Michelle died of polio. I'm alive and healthy and do a

very good job! I'm here because I want to help Sister Faith, and I am *not* your sister to be ordered about!'

'Meryl said . . .' he began.

'Meryl isn't here,' said Rebecca. 'Meryl would be furious if she found us together, and she's far more suitable for you than a copy of your sister.' She coiled her hair up and stuck in the pins viciously. 'Now, I'm Rebecca Perivale, with no long hair, and you can forget what happened. I have work to do even if you haven't.' She fixed her belt and picked up the cup to take back to the kitchen. At the door, she turned to him. 'I'm not your sister, Anthony, and personally, I've never thought of my brother as anyone I could fancy!'

'That's a terrible thing to say!' His face contorted with anger. 'At least Michelle would never say or think anything like that!'

Rebecca went out into the heat and walked slowly across to find Sister Faith. I can't stay here, she thought wildly. How can I stay when I've almost accused him of being in love with his own sister?

Sister Faith was talking to Dr Bara and they were examining a small boy with sores on his legs. His pot-belly showed all the signs of early malnutrition and his eyes were sunk deeply in his head. He was hungrily eating a piece of bread and his expression was dull.

'This has been his condition for far too long,' said Dr Bara. 'They never get over being deprived of protein as infants. We can feed him and others like him, but they're already dull-witted and lack any initiative to make their own lives. He'll eat what we give him, but could never get his own food or be of use on the farms if he had to make any decision.' He spoke in English and the boy didn't even try to listen.

'His father will take him on to the next camp tomorrow. We can do nothing more. I'll make sure they have a bottle of water and food to take,' said Sister Faith. 'May God be kind to them.' She saw Rebecca's sad expression. 'We save more than we lose and the numbers are growing, so we do good. Try not to become involved. We must keep this camp going and concentrate on the ones who will recover.'

'Your sub-cuts are doing well, Sister Becky,' said Dr Bara. 'I have four more babies to test for dysentery and then they'll need feeding. Make up more rehydration liquid with the higher potassium content, as I suspect they're lacking that and other mineral salts.'

'It's good to have you with us,' said Sister Faith, smiling. 'I hope you stay.' She regarded Rebecca with sharp eyes, noticing that she looked upset. 'If you have any problems, come straight to me.'

'No problems,' said Rebecca firmly. She set her chin at a defiant angle and went to fetch the equipment she needed.

'I'll show him that I can stay and work as hard as anyone. I'll show him that I'm not like his sister in any way. I could cut off my hair, for a start! I will not be regarded as her ghost!'

Work and meals filled the day, and even with no big convoy of new refugees, the camp was still full and many of the children needed care. By nightfall, the staff were still hard at work, by the light of fitful kerosene lamps that roared and spluttered and cast uneven light, but made it possible to carry on until the last baby was fed, the last injection given.

Gradually, as Rebecca had to ask Tony for advice, or to take him sterile drip sets, the tension between them faded. He even managed a rueful grin and gave her some sweets that were rapidly turning to sticky lumps of sugar in his pocket but were good to suck and ease the dryness that couldn't be stopped by frequent drinks.

'Dr Bara?' said Rebecca during the late evening. She handed him two packets of her chewing gum and he laughed with delight.

'I'm not asking if you can spare them. I just want to know if you have any more and when will the supply run out?'

'I have a couple of dozen packets, but I shall ration you,' she said sternly. 'You're welcome to the lot, but if you have them all now, you'll waste them.'

He chuckled. 'Allah sent you here, Sister Becky. Allah is good.'

Rebecca was touched by the offhand care he showed her. Hamid was there with fresh drinks as soon as she said she was thirsty, and fresh dates appeared like magic, with the whisper that 'My master sent them.' The work was endless and some had to be left until the next day, but by the time the staff sat down to a meal, no child had been unfed and the cries of babies from the makeshift tents could be ignored and left to the mothers.

'Meryl and Kurt would have been useful here,' said Sister Faith. 'It put an extra load on you, Becky, when you've been here for only a day.'

'I loved every minute,' said Rebecca. She ate ravenously. 'I could even get to like *foule* if I'm this hungry!' The lamb stew was appetising and the rice well cooked and the bread, freshly made in the tin oven, was delicious.

'Peel your fruit,' warned Tony as she selected a ripe peach from the box brought from Gedaref.

'Yes,' she said, 'I do peel fruit, even at home, unless I'm sure it's clean.' He reddened. 'I'm even getting used to the heat,' she said, and laughed. 'I had no idea it was possible to wash all over in such little water. It proves how much we waste at home.' She thought for a moment, then said, 'I can't think how I shall be able to wash my hair. I can't take water for that. Perhaps I should cut it short and not need to do it, just brush it well and hope for the best.'

'You mustn't do that!' Rebecca laughed and looked at the shocked faces. Everyone had said the same.

'The women of my country have to be without water for weeks, and sometimes months, but their hair is not dirty,' Dr Bara said. 'They comb it well and rub in fragrant oils, and the heat of the sun takes away any grease.'

Rebecca glanced at Tony. He too had said, impulsively, 'You mustn't cut it,' but she knew he longed to keep the memory of his dead sister alive. I wonder if that's why the other women in his family have short hair? she thought. Could they not bear to be reminded?

Hamid came in and spoke to Dr Bara in a low voice. The doctor looked stern. 'What is it?' asked Sister Faith.

'The refugees have found the old dried-up wadi again and think they can dig for water. They're camping there and refuse to move on.'

'We can't do anything tonight,' said Sister Faith, 'and there'll be no rain or floods, so they must stay there, but tomorrow we must make sure that the others leaving don't go there to join them.'

'Why not, if there's a chance of water?' asked Rebecca.

'The river beds are dry, but they're still riverbeds, and if the rains come, they'll be in spate again, and the last time it happened many were drowned.' Dr Bara looked out at the crowded camp. 'Can you imagine hundreds of people caught in a sudden tide of water, the force of which they have no idea until it hits them?'

'I can't imagine this place with rain at all,' Rebecca confessed, 'but surely they know their own country?'

'They accept what comes, and to them, death is always just round the corner,' said Tony. 'You see it in the faces of mothers who don't expect their babies to live, and in the faces of men who've had a failed harvest for the past three years and now face starvation.'

'If the rains come, what then?' asked Rebecca.

'They flock back to plant seed and to get ready for harvest,' said Dr Bara. 'It's their only hope, and we must be ready with seed corn and potatoes and mealies for them to plant.' He smiled. 'Things are better, thanks to people like us and the fact that some of the villagers now take on responsibility for their own people.' He yawned. 'Bed for everyone,' he insisted. 'We don't know if another crowd will come in the morning. It depends on the visa situation. Kurt and Meryl might be much busier than we are, and they might have to stay for a few days.'

Rebecca went alone to her hut and shut the door. It was hot and airless and she missed having another human being with her. She switched on her lamp and looked into the shadows, half expecting to see a snake or some other creature, but the walls were solid and the one window was covered with mosquito-proof gauze, as yet unnecessary but at least useful to keep out the huge moths and flying insects that would be attracted to the light.

She heard a footstep outside and called to see who was there. 'I wanted to say good night,' said Tony. There were more footsteps and a tap on the door. 'There's no need, Hamid,' said the doctor in a voice full of irritation. 'You don't guard Sister Sachs when she's alone.'

'I sleep here, Doctor. It is my master's order,' said Hamid.

'Good night,' called Tony. 'Feel quite safe. You're being protected from whatever Bara thinks might harm you!'

He went away, and Rebecca wondered if he came often to the hut when Meryl was there alone. He expected her to be alone and unprotected, so he must have been here in the past when everyone was in their own huts, and did he only say good night?

'I put fresh *lemoon* in the jug here in the cool, Sister. I say good night,' said Hamid.

'Good night, Hamid, and thank you . . . for everything,' said Rebecca.

CHAPTER SEVEN

'MERYL and Kurt have been gone for three days,' said Sister Faith. She looked at the others gathered round the table in the half-light of dawn and pushed the dish of dates along to Tony Brent. 'I have news that some rain has fallen back there in Ethiopia and the refugees have stopped coming over the border. The authorities at the border posts are being overwhelmed by requests for seed corn, and the farmers now feel that they can work again.'

'The end shed is full of seed and farm tools,' said Dr Bara. 'With only a few left who need medical treatment, we should send what we can to the police station by the border. I have friends there who will see that the seeds are given out fairly, and we have more coming from Khartoum as soon as they can send them.'

'But surely they must be told to stay away if they have sick children?' asked Rebecca, horrified to think of all the babies being dragged back to near-starvation while the farms were tilled and sown. 'They'll need feeding while the crops grow, and who knows if the rains will be enough?'

'All this is true,' said Dr Bara patiently. 'But this is Africa, Sister Becky, and the people will sniff the air and smell rain and know that it gives life. Many children will die, including some that we have saved here, but they will go and accept what Allah sends, whether it be life or death.'

'I think Meryl and Kurt may be working much harder

than we are,' continued Sister Faith. 'The camp here is less congested now and the clinics aren't busy. I suggest that Anthony takes Rebecca and the Range Rover to find out what's happening.' She smiled and didn't miss the tense glance that Rebecca gave her. 'You can leave in an hour and come back tomorrow, bringing our supplies from the train and the news. If Meryl and Kurt are exhausted, you can relieve them and send them back here instead of returning yourself.'

'What if you get busy again?' asked Rebecca.

'Not for a day or so,' stated Dr Bara. 'Even if there are hundreds on the way, and I doubt it verra much, they will not arrive for days, after the delay in giving out visas, and now the congestion at the border with many going back to their own villages.' He looked serious, and exchanged glances with Sister Faith. 'My main concern is with the people camped in the dry wadi. Find out how much rain fell and where, and I must persuade them to put their tents high and out of the wadi bed, in case of flood.'

'You will go?' It was question and order, and Rebecca nodded.

'Yes, Sister Faith. If that's what you want, I'll go,' she said. She avoided looking at Tony Brent, knowing that this arrangement would not be popular with him, but unable to trust her own expression. The thought of travelling with him alone filled her with a kind of exquisite dread that made her spine tingle where once his hand had lingered. Their work over the past few days had not thrown them together alone, as there had been a steady stream of inoculations and blood tests for him and sterilising and feeding babies for her, in a hut where many came and went and some of the other nuns worked all day.

Hamid put down a mat and slept across her door at night, and Tony had not come to the hut again to say good night. Rebecca looked up and saw Dr Bara's expression. He was angry for some reason.

'I thought Hamid could go and take one of the men from the camp with him. He could take a family of mother, father and two children as well, to help them on the way back,' he said, with a proud stiffness that Rebecca had only suspected would come to the surface if he was annoyed.

'We need Hamid for so many things,' said Sister Faith gently. 'He can't be spared, as most of my nuns speak nothing of the local dialects, and he has the respect of all the refugees.'

'Is it right to send a man and a woman together?' asked Dr Bara. 'Your church and mine agree on some things, Sister Faith.'

'But we trust,' said Sister Faith simply. 'You made no objection to Kurt and Meryl going together.'

'That's different,' he said coldly. 'She doesn't matter.'

Rebecca wished the ground would open beneath her. Everyone was talking across her as if she didn't exist. She glanced at Tony and saw that his face had paled under the tan and his cheek was tense. He controlled his voice and it came deep and full of submerged anger. 'You can send one of your men to sleep at Sister Perivale's door, or Sister Faith can send a nun to chaperon us if you think that of me,' he said in a grating voice.

'You're a man,' said Dr Bara, and smiled. 'And you're angry because you have thoughts that you wish to hide.' He clapped his hands and Hamid came into the room. He spoke rapidly in Arabic and Hamid listened, his face giving no hint to his reaction or what was said. He made the slight obeisance that was customary and left the room.

'I've told Hamid to help you get ready and he will check the oil and gas in the Range Rover. He will also fill your water tanks and ask the women in the kitchens to pack food for your stay.'

'Thank you, Gamel,' said Tony, and Rebecca sensed a lessening of tension between the men. 'I'll take care of her and see that the Range Rover comes to no harm too,' he added, with a wry smile.

The Sudanese doctor nodded gravely. 'I believe you, Tony,' he said. 'I accept your word.'

Rebecca looked away, feeling like a teenage girl who was being sent on an errand but couldn't be trusted to do it alone. What was worse, Dr Bara seemed to have the idea that she was in some kind of danger with Tony and that she might expect the same lack of respect that Meryl managed to generate among the men she met.

That made Tony into a man who would seduce any woman he could find alone, even a girl he thought of as a pale replica of his beloved and now, to Rebecca, sickening little sister!

'I'll pack some things,' she murmured, and fled to her hut.

'May I help?' Sister Faith stood in the doorway. 'Take enough for three days,' she said. 'You may be back tomorrow, but nothing is certain. Be sure to take water purifying tablets, and use them carefully.' She hovered near the bed and looked uneasy. 'I hope all will be well.' She walked to the window and gazed at the green mosquito screen. 'Am I right to send you, Becky? Was I right to make you come here?'

'You were right,' said Rebecca with more firmness

than she felt. 'I've learned a lot here, and I'm sure I can cope with most emergencies.'

'Most,' said Sister Faith. 'I'm a nun and can see only the good in the men who work here, but Dr Bara is a man, and as a man can read the minds of other men, in matters that never touch me.'

'He's Sudanese, in spite of his accent,' said Rebecca. 'The Sudanese have a very different attitude to women and think that two people alone must be involved as the man has animal instincts and no respect for a female. They have their women circumcised so that they can never have pleasure in sex and exist for man's pleasure alone.' She spoke bluntly, tired of all the undercurrent of conjecture. 'I can say no, loud and clear, Sister, and Anthony Brent has an idea that I'm . . . like his sister.' She found it unnecessary to describe the passion she had sensed that fought with his protective instincts, and she thrust away the knowledge that if he did attempt to make love to her, she might not be able to resist him.

'You're right, Becky.' The nun smiled. 'Good luck, and God bless you. Come back safely.'

The last item went into the pack and Rebecca changed into trousers and shirt and safari boots. Her hair was tightly plaited in a coil and her linen hat sat straight on her head. I look like the woman in *The African Queen*, she thought with grim satisfaction.

She smiled. Even that awful little creep that Paul had taken her to meet wouldn't fancy her now, so she was safe with Tony Brent.

'Amusing?' asked Tony as he slid into the Range Rover beside her.

'I was just thinking how far we are away from Beattie's,' she told him.

'And all the people there? I'm sure you miss them, or some people?'

'I miss my friends,' she replied. 'I wonder how Meryl has managed?'

'In what way?' His glance was wary.

'With supplies,' she answered innocently. 'They went for one day and may have had to eat local food.'

'Yes, I hadn't thought of that. We may do too, but Hamid put in a Primus stove and mealie meal and dried meat and plenty of water, so even if we stay, we can exist safely.' He settled at the wheel, and Rebecca stifled a smile. He had been very edgy when he thought she meant Meryl and Kurt together. It must have hurt his pride and manhood to have Dr Bara hint that Meryl, the woman he loved, was no more than a tart.

The sun gained height and strength and by noon they were still far enough away from their destination to need a rest and refreshment. Tony brought out an awning that hitched on to the side of the vehicle and gave them welcome shade only slightly marred by the smell of Diesel oil.

Rebecca took some of the food from the cooler box and they ate cold lamb and bread and tomatoes and drank *lemoon*. 'People pay a fortune to picnic on safari in Africa,' she said lazily.

'And we have all this for nothing,' he replied, laughing.

'The romance of Africa!' said Rebecca, as if doing a commercial. 'Come to Africa and see the desert, the wide open spaces, the wild animals . . . are there wild animals?' Her eyes widened and she became aware of the vast distances and the shimmering heat. On the horizon was a wide clump of trees where a well might be hidden.

'Take a look.' Tony brought powerful binoculars from the car and sat beside her on the rug. He scanned the distance and gave a shout. 'Giraffe!'

Rebecca took the glasses. 'Where?' All she could see were the trees and some blobs that might be anything.

'To the left,' he instructed her, and she gasped. It was like a revelation. Out of the heat haze she saw them, and beyond, some kind of gazelles.

He guided her hands to focus on more animals and held them with his own. Rebecca breathed deeply and hoped he couldn't feel the beating of her heart as his arm rested on her breast. 'It's exciting!' she breathed.

'Yes, exciting,' he whispered. His lips traced a sensual line over her cheeks and lips and chin and on to the sweet cleft of her throat, and the glasses slipped from her hands. Her hat fell off and he caressed the tender escaping tresses that were too short to stay pinned in the heat. Rebecca closed her eyes. This was heaven and hell mixed. This was what she wanted and dreaded. This was the beat of the desert and the primitive song of desire. Tony's lips were firm and warm and his mouth sent a message of deep sexuality into hers, arousing her to bring her arms round him and her hands to seize the dark hair at the nape of his neck and draw him closer in a kiss that seemed to cry out in its intensity.

'Becky,' he murmured. 'Darling little Becky!'

Her fingers found the base of his hair and the large mound that showed the love of women and the love of family. He could be hers for a while, now, if she encouraged him. He could be a wonderful lover, husband or companion if she had the right, but he was in love with Meryl.

She pushed him away, gently but firmly. 'No,' she whispered. 'You have no right.'

Tony came out of a trance that had held all the colours of paradise and stared at her. 'I want you so much,' he said softly. 'I want you so much, Becky.'

'No,' she said again, and turned away so that her traitorous eyes wouldn't show him her love. She buttoned up the shirt that had opened to his exploring, hypnotic hand and felt a pain where his kiss had lingered on her breast.

'You're not free.' His voice was flat and his eyes showed hurt pride and frustration. 'I forgot Paul Weldon; and so did you,' he added accusingly.

'Yes, I forgot,' Rebecca agreed, recovering. 'Out here, I could forget many things and many people, but we have to go back and face our . . . responsibilities.' Her heart was crying, 'And you, my darling, have to go back to Meryl who claims you for her own.' Let him think it was the memory of Paul that made her resist him, but she knew now that Dr Bara was right. He knew men and knew what would happen even if Tony was promised in love to a woman.

She recalled Meryl, first with heavy make-up and then with the wet tee-shirt clinging to her body, and knew that to Anthony Brent, all women must be as Meryl was, easy with her behaviour and with her favours. Did he accept the fact that she was probably sleeping with Kurt? Was lovemaking just another release of an appetite? Like a good meal?

'I'm sorry. I know you, and I was a fool.' Tony gave a short laugh. 'At times, when you have your hair down, I long to protect you as I would have done Michelle, my sister. You look so vulnerable and so sweet, but today you sat beside me all the way and I saw a woman, a very desirable woman, in spite of that ghastly hat.' He shrugged with mock resignation. 'I'm all mixed up. Lead me to a good shrink!'

'And you did promise Dr Bara to look after me,' she replied, also mocking, in a little-girl voice.

'Damn Gamel!' he said, and began to stow away the awning.

In five minutes they were driving again, with the heat of the sun once more beating down on the roof and the eddies of dust spurting up from under the wheels. Soon they saw the camps outside the town and a water-van making the rounds with fresh water, but they didn't stop and had to pick a way between handcarts and families sitting in the middle of the road.

'I'll go straight to the Mission, and we can leave the Rover until I contact Kurt and Bara's friends,' said Tony.

'There's a Mission here?' Rebecca looked surprised. 'I thought Meryl said they'd have no place to sleep except the truck.' She put a hand over her mouth. 'I must have misunderstood,' she said weakly.

'I doubt it,' said Tony grimly. 'I'm afraid Meryl has a great need for male company.'

'Don't you mind?' she asked. He shrugged and didn't reply. A man shouted and two tall Sudanese clambered on to the back of the vehicle.

'These are Bara's contacts,' said Tony. He spoke to them in slow but obviously understandable dialect and they replied.

'They say Meryl and Kurt are at the Mission, so we can see them at the same time,' said Anthony.

'Great,' murmured Rebecca. The heat and the rough road and her own mixed-up emotions made her feel limp.

It was fast approaching dusk and the lights from the low one-storey building on the outskirts of the town came on, one by one. Rebecca sighed with relief as they got out of the car and went into the main entrance, pushing a way through a crowd who waited silently for food.

A child ran to Rebecca and held her hand. It was one she had fought to save a few days ago and it now looked well-fed and smiling. Rebecca laughed and pushed a sweet into the tiny hand, then put a finger to her lips. If the child spread the news that there were sweets being given away, there would be a flood of hands extended that couldn't be filled.

They went in to find the Sister in Charge and there were more children waiting to be inoculated. 'They have their hands full,' said Tony. 'This is another batch who came before the news of the rains broke.'

'I saw some from our camp,' said Rebecca.

'Pointless, isn't it?' he said bitterly. 'We worked on them and now they insist on going back where there's cholera, hard work and near-starvation again.'

'They might make it,' she said comfortingly, and he gave her a tired smile.

'I think we shall be busy,' he said after speaking to the Canadian doctor who had asked them into his office. 'Meryl went down with dysentery this morning and Kurt was ill yesterday.'

'Oh, no!' Rebecca looked at the doctor. 'Where are they? Can I see them?'

'Both asleep,' he said briefly. 'They've had all the usual anti-nauseants and some atropine, and now we wait until the fluids are replaced. They'll be fine, but not much use to me just now. How do you feel? We have that lot to get through tonight.'

'I think our friends haven't made a very good impression,' murmured Anthony.

'A bit like when I was training. It was a sin for a nurse to be ill!' said Rebecca. 'We hadn't a lot of sympathy shown us when we fell by the wayside.'

'Even at Beattie's? I *am* surprised,' he said.

The doctor hurried back with a box of inoculations and syringes. Without another word, Rebecca rolled up her shirt sleeves and washed her hands at the sink, then she took her place at the table where a line of children held by mothers waited. She smiled, and forced down her weariness. One by one she injected and made notes and put the required rubber band round the wrist to show that the treatment was done, then waved the mother away to the food queue.

The line went on and on, and the routine was so monotonous that she felt that she could never stop, but would go on swabbing an arm, smiling at the mother and injecting, even after she fell asleep.

A Sudanese nurse kept her supplied with sterile syringes and swabs, and at last the room was empty of patients and Rebecca stretched every muscle in her back.

A nun touched her arm and asked her come and eat. She smiled, and as soon as Rebecca entered the dining room, she sensed the warmth of welcome. The Canadian grinned. 'I don't know where you're from, but please stay, lady!' Tony came in soon after and sank into a seat. 'We had them cook for you and me and Sister here,' said the Canadian. 'I've got some Kirkady if you like it, and then I suggest you both crash out in that room over there. You must be bushed.'

'What about Meryl?' asked Rebecca, eating ravenously.

'She's all right. I'm Don Maine, by the way. No, they can go back tomorrow. I'll dose them up and they can

take the ambulance they brought with them.' He eyed
Rebecca from under shaggy brows. 'Only themselves to
blame for this. Meryl brought in some food from the
market and didn't wash it, or cook it, or do something to
make it pure. Whatever, it's given them both the runs
and they feel lousy. Bad luck on them, but worse for us,
trying to cope and thinking we had extra hands.'

'They sleep here?' queried Tony.

'Sure! Where else?'

'You might have been full up,' said Tony, and
Rebecca knew he hated the thought of Meryl lying in the
ambulance, making love with Kurt.

'No, Kurt made sure of beds before they started to
work here,' Don smiled. 'They worked hard at first, I'll
give them that, but it's such a waste of time if they're ill.'

'And have you finished with us tonight?' asked Tony.
'I suspect you're one bloody slave-driver!'

'I am—oh yes, I am.' Don seemed to think it was
hilarious. 'Get some sleep—and thanks, both of you.'

'Where do I sleep?' asked Rebecca. The room was as
big as her hut, but in it were two camp beds.

'Here,' said Tony. 'Don't worry. You don't need
Hamid to protect you tonight. I couldn't rise to any
occasion just now.'

Rebecca washed in the cubicle outside the room, and
noticed that Tony stayed away until she was in bed. She
lay on top of the bed with her hair loose, and dressed in a
cotton dress so that if she was needed, she was ready to
appear in public and, more important, ready to be seen
by Anthony Brent.

She closed her eyes when he came into the room and
he took off his shirt. She watched under half-closed lids
as he unzipped his trousers and slipped out of them. Her
heart beat unsteadily. Had he decided he was not as tired

as all that? In the light from the lamp by the door, she saw his long firm legs and muscular thighs. His tiny briefs hid nothing of the outline of his masculine form and his waist was flat-stomached and flowed up to firm pectorals that showed a darkness of curling hair. She wished she had turned over before he came into the room, so she wouldn't see him, but it was too late, and she knew that this vision would remain with her long after he had forgotten her and was making love to Meryl. Now she realised that he had not stayed away out of modesty, but so that he could go to Meryl and see that she was all right.

His shadow lengthened and came towards her bed like a batwing against the moon. It stopped, and Rebecca tried to breathe evenly and deeply as if she was asleep. The scent of coarse soap and a male body came nearer, and she wanted to open her eyes, hold out her arms and draw him on to the bed with her, but she remained silent and still.

In the distance children cried and women crooned songs of hope and despair and sorrow, and the African night lay dark and mysterious over the camp. Tony picked up a strand of the soft brown hair rippling over the pillow and held it to his lips. Rebecca turned away, burying her face and biting her lip to prevent the cry that wanted to echo the moans of the women.

He stepped back and stood watching her, but she stayed as she was, her knees drawn up and her head tucked in like a child in the womb. Tony walked to his own bed and flung himself on it so that the poor springs shuddered. From her cocoon of hair, with every nerve raw and tuned to his voice, Rebecca heard him say, 'Damn Bara!'

Long after the steady breathing had deepened and

Tony slept the sleep of the totally exhausted, Rebecca watched the trail of lights on the ceiling as fires were lit and doused, trucks came and went and the life of the town went on as if it was noon, but she too sank into oblivion and was shocked when the alarm by her bed shrilled and she pushed back her hair and saw the dawn.

'Only four hours' sleep!' she groaned, and remembered where she was. She looked across at the empty bed and around the hut. The one sheet was neatly folded and Tony's towel was gone from the hook by the window. She picked up her own towel and her daytime clothes and wandered across to the washroom. In the dim light, people were hurrying back to huts, and outside the barrier that cut off the staff from the public was a shadow that moved and became a group of Ethiopians, patiently waiting for the Mission to feed them.

'Here we go again!' Tony sat on his bed and looked up as Rebecca entered the hut. He laughed, 'You look grim enough to fight a war!' His face was relaxed after a deep sleep and his eyes were clear and regarded her with amused affection. 'You really are a bit schitzo,' he told her. 'Last night I wanted to tuck you up with a teddy bear, and now you're Sister Rebecca Perivale, ready for action.'

'We're fighting a war,' said Rebecca. 'And I never did like teddy bears.' She laughed and locked her bag in the chest beside her bed. He would never know how close she had come to asking one shaggy teddy bear into her bed last night. 'I'm hungry. I suppose the others have been up for hours,' she said.

'No, they're gathering,' said Tony.

'How's Meryl? I must see her this morning.'

'I peeped in, but she was asleep and Kurt was looking a bit drained but on his feet. They'll go back today and

rest up in the other Mission and leave us to cope here.'
He grinned. 'Don't look so worried! It isn't as busy as
last night, and we should follow them in another day or
two at the most.'

'I don't mind hard work,' she assured him.

'I know.' Tony looked at her seriously. 'When you
said you were coming here, I thought you'd flake out in a
day, but I begin to believe you're far stronger than it
appears. You work as hard as anyone and still manage to
look as if . . . as if . . .'

'As if what?' she asked softly.

'As if you could take out five Guinea Worms this
morning,' he added, with a wicked smile.

Rebecca blushed, knowing from his expression that
he had almost paid her a compliment and then changed
his mind. 'Great! May I have breakfast first? I do like a
man who keeps his promises, and you did promise me
Guinea Worms in Africa.'

Breakfast was made up of hardboiled eggs, Arab
bread and mangoes. The coffee was surprisingly good,
thanks to Don who had supplies sent from home and
swore he couldn't function without fresh coffee even in
the desert. 'Not too bad today,' he said. 'Some have
gone back the way they came as they've heard of good
rains and full waterholes. We expect more seeds and
plants on the train this morning, and the police have set
up a compound where it will be sorted out and rationed
to all men with a bona fide piece of land.'

'I did notice the goats,' said Rebecca, wrinkling her
nose.

'We keep them here for our own use and sell the kids,
so there'll be some for the farmers,' said Don. 'You can
understand them wanting to go home. We all get like
that and here more than most places,' he added with

feeling. 'I dream of fishing and breathing the cold air up north, and eating lobster and salads and drinking . . .'

'Don't!' shuddered Tony. 'I just want to get back to our own camp for a start.'

'Yeah.' Don sipped his coffee and looked thoughtful. 'A pity Meryl is like this. You could have swopped with her, Rebecca, and she could have stayed here with Tony.'

'Willingly,' said Rebecca, in a level voice.

'A pity it wasn't arranged like that, but I suppose the nuns had no idea and wouldn't go for it in any case,' Don went on. He laughed. 'They're out of this world in more senses than one. Wonderful women, but they have no idea of what goes on under their noses.'

'What do you want me to do first?' asked Rebecca. She stood up and brushed the crumbs from her shirt. She looked at Tony steadily. 'I think you said I had a date with a worm!'

Yesterday she could almost believe that he loved her. Love, she thought, was far from desire and the immediate need to slake a thirst, and he had Meryl for that particular satisfaction.

'Wash your eyes with cool water, Sister,' said one of the nuns later. 'You look as if the sand has irritated them, and you don't want to get trachoma, do you?'

'I'll do that,' said Rebecca, but she didn't say that the smarting came from behind the eyes and deep in her heart, and not from the burning sand, but it gave her an excuse for reddened eyes. Did the whole of the medical team know that Tony and Meryl were lovers? Did Meryl tell everyone she met of their liaison? I thought men were the ones who boasted of conquests, she thought, and that women hid it until it was so blatant that nobody could fail to guess.

She bathed her eyes and put light-textured cream on the eyelids, and felt better. Her mask hid any facial expression and her eyes, now turned towards her work, were enigmatic. The simple tray of scalpel, tweezers and nylon sutures and holder, with swabs for antiseptic and small adhesive dressings, was all she needed for her morning's task, and as she gained confidence, she managed to make only tiny incisions to take out the worm that had worked its way to the surface and caused pain and inflammation.

Once more she sprayed on the local anaesthetic to freeze the affected area, waited for a while to allow it to take and then quickly incised, swabbed and seized the tiny cause of the bother. Sometimes a stitch wasn't necessary and could be closed with the dressing, but once a badly inflamed area made her go to find Don to ask his advice.

'Tony!' he called. 'Can you come?' and left Rebecca with the one she wanted to avoid.

'Too much for you?' asked Tony. 'How many are there? You should have called me earlier, but I thought you wanted to try one.' He smiled indulgently. 'It was a bit much to expect a girl like you to do them.'

'This is the last one,' she said coldly. 'I've removed nine this morning, but this one is close to a prominent vein and I wanted Don to see it.'

'Nine?' He eyed her calm face and steady hands and flushed. 'I'm sorry, I had no idea. I really thought you'd chicken out, but you've done a fine job.' The words came with an effort as if he wished she was stupid and fragile, and couldn't come to terms with the other Rebecca.

'Well, do I go in after it here, or from the other end of

the swelling away from the vein but making a bigger incision?'

'The bigger incision,' he said. 'You may need an artery forceps if you have to go deep.' The man sat impassively on the stool and made no sign of pain or discomfort when the doctor carefully cut the skin while Rebecca stemmed the flow of blood from a small vein under the surface. The tiny operation was over in five minutes, with the cavity cleared and swabbed and treated with sulphonamide powder and stitched with absorbable sutures so that the dressing could be left on, until it wore off and no further treatment would be necessary.

'Thank you,' said Rebecca.

'No, I should thank you,' he said, and once more he looked slightly puzzled as if she was indeed two people. 'I wish I had someone like you in my clinic in London,' he added.

'Guinea Worms are a bit thin on the ground in Mayfair and Bart's, aren't they?' she said sweetly. 'What next?'

'Refreshment,' he said firmly. 'You haven't had your fluid quota for the morning.' He looked sideways at her as they walked to the rest hut. 'You must be tired.'

'Not at all. I think I'm beginning to like the heat, and that was interesting. I've gone off feeding babies.'

'Finished?' asked Don laconically.

'All done,' said Rebecca. 'I had some help with the last one, but the rest were easy. I burned all the gunge and the line-up isn't bad now for food and inoculations.'

'I knew you'd be fine,' he said. He turned to Tony. 'Choose the small girls who look as if a breeze would blow them away. Choose them every time. They're tough, believe me. Never be fooled by that little-girl look! I married one, and I should know. She's in Cairo just now with the three kids, but she's coming over next week.' He leaned over the table and toasted her with his *lemoon*. 'Great stuff. You remind me of Daisy.'

'I seem to be a clone for so many people,' said Rebecca. 'I *am* a person in my own right.' She smiled at Don but sensed that the man at her side was taking in every word.

'Well, tough or not, you rest now. You had no sleep last night,' said Don firmly.

'As soon as my head touched the pillow,' she lied, 'but I could do with a rest.'

'Tony, can you help me with one case in theatre? It will take half an hour and then you can go for your rest, too.' Don came back from the door. 'You saw Meryl before she left?' Tony nodded. 'Good. Pity you couldn't go with her, but Kurt seems a good guy.'

Rebecca sank on to her bed and knew she was bone-weary. Her eyes closed, and this time she did sleep as soon as her head touched the pillow, and lay oblivious to everything outside the hut until one of the nuns came to call her. Only then did she know that at some time Tony had come in too and now lay fast asleep with his shirt off and his head back in an attitude of complete ease and deep sleep. One arm hung over the edge of the bed and his fingers touched the ground.

The nun smiled and pointed to the other cup on the small tray as if she would prefer that Rebecca woke the man on the bed and gave him his coffee.

'Has he had enough rest?' whispered Rebecca. The nun nodded and left, leaving Tony asleep. Rebecca went to the bed and touched the firm shoulder, but as he made no response she had to shake him gently.

The arm looked uncomfortable, so she took it to fold across his chest. The strong face remained in repose, and she looked down at him, taking her fill of the sight. Soon she would go back to London, and if they met it would be fully clothed in an operating theatre, or at a social event at the hospital . . . if Tony bothered to come back to Beattie's once he had his clinics full at Bart's and his private work organised in the hospital at Westminster. His mouth showed arrogance and yet the corners, even in sleep, were upturned in gentle humour, and his dark hair clung damply to his brow, after a brief sluicing in cold water before he came to bed.

Rebecca bent towards him, drawn by a bond that was filled with sad sweetness. Meryl would never fill his mind as well as his bed, and yet claimed him, publicly and without shame. Impulsively, Rebecca kissed his cheek and wished he loved her.

A firm hand seized her wrist, and she tried to jump back from the bed. 'That's quite the sweetest wakening I've ever had,' said Tony. 'Now I know what it must have been like to be wakened after a hundred years by a lovely maiden.'

'Rip van Winkle wasn't wakened by a maiden, and it was a prince who came and woke the Sleeping Beauty,' said Rebecca. Her blush couldn't be controlled. 'I shook you and poked your arm, then wondered if you really were asleep,' she lied. 'That was my last resort. I only use it on very stubborn cases.' She tried to pull away. 'One of the nuns brought coffee and she'll be back for the cups,' she warned.

'I'm still half asleep,' he said, and with one sweep of his arm, she was clutched to his bare chest and his lips found hers. She struggled and he released her, watching her brush down her cotton dress and then touch her hair. He laughed, and the sound was musical, and if she could have stayed with him, would have made an echo of warmth and closeness with her own heart.

'I must go,' she said with as much dignity as she could command. 'Don will need me.'

'Don can wait.' Tony swung his legs over the side of the camp bed and Rebecca ran from the hut. 'Fool!' she muttered as she went to find Don. 'What did you expect? And now he thinks you're asking for sex, just as Meryl would do, leading a man on and showing that she wants him.'

'Talking to yourself?' Don stepped out of the shade of one of the outbuildings. 'Must be the heat.'

'You look worried,' she said, and knew something was wrong.

'You and Tony must go back to warn them at the Mission. Heavy rains are falling and the rivers are filling fast. One camp was inundated during the night and a lot of people were drowned. It gave no warning, but burst the banks of a river that had been dry for two years and swept everything in its path.'

'You think it will come this far?' asked Rebecca.

'By tomorrow, it will fill the river-bed down in that small valley, and by the next day it will reach you and fill all the dried-up wadis.' Don looked towards the heavy clouds that hung over the horizon. 'Listen!'

Dull rumbles followed by the cutting edge of lightning came over the parched ground, and from the crowd of families waiting to be fed came a shout and there was movement everywhere as they gathered up bundles and children and goats if they possessed them, and filled water bottles from the huge cans drawn from the well. Three policemen were shouting and even threatening them in an effort to make them stay, but the growing column of refugees turned to face their homeland and water, the chance to grow crops and regain their farms.

'It's hopeless,' sighed Don. 'Nothing can stop them going back, and even the police can do little as this batch have been waiting for visas to go on to Gedaref and haven't been accepted as yet, so they can go back the way they came.'

'Are there supplies for Sister Faith?' asked Rebecca crisply. 'I'll pack and supervise the loading—and would you tell Tony? He's only just waking up.'

'I'm here,' said a quiet voice behind her. 'Pack my bag, Rebecca. I'll stay here, as I can communicate better than you.'

She left him with Don and hurried to get the two small bags packed, and by the time she had them in the Range Rover, the water and Diesel had been topped up and the cartons of stores loaded. There was no time for lengthy goodbyes, but Don gave her a big hug and told her to take care.

'One in a million!' he called after her as she swung up into her seat. 'Take care of her, Tony. Girls like that don't grow on trees.'

'No, I hadn't noticed any,' called Tony. He smiled briefly. 'Hang on to that awful hat! We have to hurry.'

The vehicle bucked and bounced and Rebecca clenched her teeth to stop herself from crying out, but the man at the wheel sat impassively, avoiding the worst of the obstructions in the dirt roads.

Groups of Ethiopians wandered down the path without any obvious haste, but smiled as they looked at the dense cloud over their homes. Thunder still growled and the herds of antelope in the distance now stood trembling or rushed away from the sound. Rebecca took some fruit from a box and managed to peel it, but ripe mangoes are messy things, and by the time she handed portions to Tony to eat while he drove, they were juicy and sent droplets of sweetness over the steering wheel.

'Great,' he said, after gulping a piece. 'More, please.' He glanced at her. 'We can't stop for a picnic, however much we might enjoy it.' Her cheeks burned. Did he think she wanted to lie with him under the awning and make love? Did he now, after her one innocent and gentle kiss, think that it opened the flood gates to passion? The cloying sweetness of the fruit filled her mouth but not her empty heart. If the floods came, her work would be over and she could go home.

CHAPTER EIGHT

REBECCA stumbled from the Range Rover, aching in every fibre of her body and her hands sticky with fruit juice. She reached back for her own pack, then decided to wash her hands first. A few flies gathered over the remnants of the food that she had managed to find among the packages and had handed to Tony as he drove. She brushed them away and wondered why there were more in the camp than she recalled earlier.

Tony followed her to the wash area to clean up before seeing Sister Faith, and they went back to the Range Rover in silence to unpack.

The camp was almost empty, and it was only when they went into the staff hut that they saw any of the nuns. Sister Faith came towards them, smiling, and took Rebecca's hand. 'Safe and well!' she said, with satisfaction. 'Meryl and Kurt are better too and will be back at work tomorrow.' She looked at Tony. 'Have they nothing for you to do back there?'

'We came to warn you, Sister.' His voice sounded as if the desert had crept into his throat. 'We can expect floods tomorrow. There's heavy rain and flooding over the border and the wadis are filling. One river burst its banks and drowned several families, so we must get the families out of the dried river beds.'

'Not easy,' said Dr Bara, who had come in and was listening. 'We tried to persuade them to come down from the wadi, but they found water and refused to move, but went even higher towards Khartoum, and to the land near the banks of the Nile.'

'We must get to them and tell them to come here where the floods won't reach them,' said Tony.

'You'll do nothing until you've eaten and rested,' said Sister Faith. 'You must have come like the wind, to get here so soon.'

'That car is no magic carpet,' said Rebecca. 'I'll never grumble that my car at home lacks a certain springiness again!' She rubbed her seat and flexed her arms.

'Eat and drink,' urged Sister Faith. 'Hamid shall take the truck to warn the people, and you must rest.' She walked outside and sniffed the air. 'It's coming,' she agreed, and hurried away to the clinic, coming back with packages of drugs. 'Take these, and each of you be responsible for your own. With water, we shall have mosquitoes and must take precautions before they arrive, or the drugs won't be effective. Take a dose now,' she ordered, and hurried away to give out anti-malarial tablets to all her nuns and the other workers.

'She's right,' said Tony, opening his package. 'Take a first dose of four tablets and then two more in six hours, and after that one twice daily.' He looked serious. 'That's the dosage for someone who's been bitten by the malaria-bearing mosquito and not the usual dose to keep the drug in the blood and so prevent infection, but as we haven't time to give it early, I advise a heavier dose now, and we can go on to the back-up dosage of one tablet a day in a week or so.'

Rebecca swallowed her tablets and drank some Kirkady, then sat down to eat lamb and rice and more fruit. Tony had eaten and left, quietly, as if he had something on his mind, and Rebecca suddenly remembered Meryl and Kurt. She finished her food and walked stiffly to the medical huts and asked where they were. One of the helpers pointed to a small hut and Rebecca went inside.

Kurt was on his bed, reading. He looked pale and thinner but cheerful. 'Not you too?' he asked. 'When did you come back?'

'We're fine,' she reassured him. 'They wanted us to come back to warn the people of floods that may be here by tomorrow.'

'Floods?' He sat up and put aside his book. 'Did you tell Meryl?'

'No, I haven't seen her. Sister Faith made us eat and take anti-malaria pills.'

'She's in the next hut. She's fine, but wobbly still, and she can start work tomorrow when I do. I must get some tablets too. I did take a course, but I used all mine, and there was no need to follow up when everything was so dry.'

He put on his shoes, and Rebecca walked to the next hut.

'Back already?' said Meryl in a mocking voice. Her face was thinner and her eyes seemed to stand out of her head like those of the dehydrated children.

'Are you better?' asked Rebecca in an effort to be friendly and to ignore the hostility in the other girl's eyes.

'I'm recovering,' said Meryl. 'What happened? The pace get too hot for you, or didn't Tony fancy you enough to make the whole romantic trip worth while?'

'I don't know what you mean, Meryl. Sister Faith told us to go to the town and we helped Don and the others as they were busy and came back here to report.' Rebecca tried to laugh. 'If I never sit in that Range Rover again on desert roads, it'll be too soon! We must have come really fast.'

'No stops for a nice picnic? No lazing under the awning on the way?'

Rebecca flushed. 'We stopped on the way out,' she admitted. 'We stopped for long enough to eat and then went on—but if you're insinuating what I think you are, forget it. Tony isn't interested in me.'

'Well, that's a relief,' said Meryl. 'I took one look at you and thought you were trouble. I'd hate to lose him now.' She shrugged. 'Sorry but men like Kurt take sex easily and make me believe they're all like that.' Her eyes were wary, and Rebecca didn't rise to the bait offered. She wants to know if either of the men have been making passes at me, she thought. If both men were interested in Meryl, then it was just lucky that Africa was fast losing its charm and she could soon go home and try to forget Anthony Brent.

'Kurt looks a bit thin, and so do you,' she said. 'Can I get you anything?'

'Only Tony. Tell him I want to see him,' Meryl replied pettishly. 'He popped his head round the door, then went away again. He must have eaten by now.'

'I'll ask him to bring you your anti-malaria tablets,' said Rebecca. 'We expect floods soon.'

But as she left the hut, she saw Tony striding towards the clinical area, followed by a small group of children, ready for inoculation. She smiled. Perhaps Meryl was right. Passion could wait until he was ready, and if he had other things to do, then even the woman he loved must wait for him to come to her. Her eyes became dreamy. Passion with Tony would be swift and deep and soul-destroying, a magical experience that could ruin a girl's life if he just used her and went away, bringing rapture followed by deep despair. She shuddered, knowing how close she had come to that rapture, that despair.

'Becky?' Sister Faith called. 'Oh, there you are. Take these pills to Meryl and tell her walk about a bit to get some strength in her legs.'

'She asked for Tony,' said Rebecca.

'She'll have to wait. He has better things to do just now. He can't spend all the day chatting to her. She's better and ought to be thinking of tomorrow, when we shall be busy.' Sister Faith handed over the malaria pills and went back to the dispensary. Rebecca walked slowly back to Meryl and gave her the pills.

'You didn't give my message,' said Meryl in an accusing tone.

'He's busy with the children,' said Rebecca simply.

'I'll go and see him there.' Meryl slipped her shoes on and walked unsteadily to the door.

'Sister did suggest a walk for you,' said Rebecca. 'Want any help? What about a walking stick? There are some long pieces of wood by the incinerator.'

'Thank you, I can manage,' said Meryl. 'I'm sure you must be very busy, giving out the pills,' she added in a pointed fashion.

She walked away under the hot sun, and Rebecca felt sorry for her. If she was in love with Tony and he with her, then of course they wanted to be together, but this anxiety showed a certain uneasiness as if Meryl thought she must make the running.

Rebecca fetched a bucket of water and locked her hut door before stripping off and washing all over. The tepid water was soothing and restored her calm, and she examined her body for insects bites or scratches as they could become infected easily in the heat and sandy conditions. The place where the splinter had been had healed and she had only a few bruises from her jolting in the vehicle. She put on a thin cotton dress over clean underwear and wished she could wear something less utilitarian on her feet, but wisely kept to the solid shoes she had been wearing in the camp. Her hair felt hot and she longed to shampoo it and brush it out into a cloud, but she had so little water that she dared not attempt it.

The small bottle that Dr Bara had given her was still in her pack, and she opened it curiously. A smell of fresh jasmine came from it and she poured a little of the oil on to her hand before rubbing it into her scalp. The heady perfume surrounded her in sensuous waves, and she felt dreamy and languorous. She brushed her hair vigorously to get rid of the scent, but it only spread the oil to the tips of the long tresses, and the perfume remained.

The brush picked up dust and her hair began to feel clean and looked wonderfully glossy when she coiled it up again in the severe knot. I shall have to stay in the fresh air and let the scent go away, she thought. If Sudanese women wore that, they must expect men to be attracted, she thought, and was surprised that Dr Bara, with his rigid views on the relationship between men and women, should have given her such sensual perfume.

In the open air, she couldn't smell it, and she breathed a sigh of relief. Her hair felt good and she could now concentrate on her work. 'You smell nice,' said Kurt, who came out of his hut as she passed.

'Is it too much? I'm used to it now, and so I don't smell it, but it's oil that Dr Bara gave me for my hair, and it does pong a bit, doesn't it?'

'Pong? My dear girl, if I were only ten per cent stronger, I'd grab you and take you to my hut! It's glorious.'

'Oh dear, Kurt, I don't know how I can get rid of it!'

'Don't try. Give us all a thrill. You'll need one of the nuns to keep an eye on you now.' He nuzzled her ear. 'My, my, I feel stronger all the time. I missed you, Becky. Too bad you had to go with Tony. He's a dry stick with women and not the man for you.'

'He's a good doctor, and that's what counts,' said Rebecca firmly.

'You're a good nurse, but you're much, much more. I brought back some whisky. Why don't we have a little reunion tonight? Just the two of us, after the rest are asleep?'

'No, Kurt. Down, boy! This scent is evil and I can't think what Dr Bara was thinking of to unleash it here, and on me of all people!'

'It's great!' laughed Kurt. 'Don't look so alarmed. I'm more talk than do, but you are rather special, Becky.' He chuckled. 'Maybe Gamel isn't immune to the English rose touch. Why else should he give you fragrant oils as if you were bound for the nuptial bed?'

'I thought you were ill! I wasted a lot of sympathy on you, Kurt, and now you seem very well indeed.'

Rebecca was still smiling when she reached the hut where Tony was finishing the treatments. He looked tired after the long drive and this sudden influx of patients, before he had rested properly. The last child was crying as the needle went in, but in another minute the smiles were back as he sucked a sweet given him from the precious and fast disappearing supply.

'I can clear this,' said Rebecca. 'Get some rest.'

'You haven't been asleep, have you?' Tony asked.

'No, just a wash and clean clothes and I'm fine,' she said, smiling. 'It makes all the difference. Collect a bucket of water when you go back to your hut.'

'I think I will.' Tony regarded her with puzzled eyes. 'You really don't look tired.' He came closer. 'Clean and scented too. I didn't think you'd bothered with duty-free scent!' He sniffed and bent to smell her hair.

'It's oil for my hair that Dr Bara gave me as I can't wash it just now,' she told him, moving away. 'It will soon wear off,' she added hopefully.

'It suits you,' he said shortly. 'But if you expect any man to get on with his work when you wear it, then you're very, very dense.' He kissed her cheek and his fingers caressed the shining hair. 'It's perfume for the night,' he whispered. 'It could send a man mad.'

'Where's Meryl?' she asked, moving away from him. 'She was looking for you.'

'Meryl?' Tony blinked. 'She came in for a minute, but I was busy and she was feeling weak, so I sent her back to her hut.'

'I took her some pills, but she asked for you,' said Rebecca.

'I'll see her on my way to my hut,' he said, and yawned. 'A bucket of water, the lady said, and I'll emerge as fresh as a daisy.' He grinned. 'Sit by me at dinner so that I can enjoy you. Makes a change from Diesel and camel dung!'

Rebecca burned all the soiled dressings and washed the syringes, putting them to boil over the spirit stove until they were sterile and she could wrap them in boiled dishes covered with gauze. She locked away the rest of the medicaments and tidied the table ready for more examinations, and by then she was feeling really tired, as if her weariness was catching up with her. She pushed back a strand of hair and once more the musky, sweet scent came to her nostrils.

'Sister Becky!' called Dr Bara. He came swiftly across

the yellow earth and his flowing robes made an arc of shadow as he moved, reminding Rebecca of the day she first saw Anthony Brent, with his gown flowing out behind him, batlike in the corridor of Beattie's. Tony Brent had looked very angry, but today this doctor looked alarmed.

'What's the matter, Dr Bara?' asked Rebecca. She glanced back to the open desert, half expecting to see a river in spate or a pride of lions.

'That bottle I gave you,' he began, then sniffed. 'Oh, no!' he exclaimed, and swore softly in pure Glaswegian.

'It cleaned my hair very well,' said Rebecca. She laughed. 'It's very strong and I'm hoping it will fade in the fresh air. Fine for off-duty, but a bit too much for working, and if I were in hospital, I'd get a rocket for wearing it.'

His face was a picture of comical dismay. 'I gave you the wrong one,' he said, and handed her another phial that looked like the one she had in her hut.

Rebecca undid the small cork and sniffed gently. The smell was soft but pleasant, but had no similarity to the opulent and sensual perfume she was wearing.

'I don't understand,' she said.

'I bought several of them for my family. I bought them in Egypt. The one that you used is meant for brides on their wedding day and is . . . slightly aphrodisiac.' He coughed in an embarrassed way, and once again Rebecca was amused at the contrast between the dark, fierce face and the Scottish voice that now sounded very ashamed.

'It will wear off,' she assured him.

'I can't think how I made the mistake,' he said. 'I was anxious to protect you when you were alone with a man, and yet I gave you that!'

'I didn't use it until I came back today,' she said in a comforting way, 'and here you can make Hamid my protector again if you think it necessary.'

'Even Hamid isn't a eunuch!' he laughed.

'I shall keep it for the purpose for which it was intended,' said Rebecca solemnly, but her eyes sparkled. 'This one I'll use tomorrow to get rid of the scent and to oil my hair. It smells like sunshine and green fields and is quite innocent.'

'Hamid has gone to the wadi, but I think we shall have to take the ambulance truck there in case of accidents. The sky is darker every minute, and soon the rains will reach us here. I'll go with Tony when he has rested.'

'You'll need a nurse or one of the nuns,' said Rebecca. 'The children respond to women better than to men.'

'Not you, Sister Becky. You stay here,' he ordered. He walked away, and Rebecca knew he wanted her to stay away from Tony until the perfume wore off. Surely he couldn't believe it had such power? But Kurt had been very interested, and if she had been wearing it in the desert . . . the journey might have had a very different ending. She made sure that the bottle was firmly closed and put it with her clothes. Some day, she thought. Some day I may need it, or I can pass it on to Nurse Frost when she gets married.

Clouds gathered and thunder once more made the camels moan. Two donkeys that stood tethered by the kitchens made such a noise that they were taken to the back of the camp and tied up in a decaying hut. The wind rose and drifts of sand on the horizon blurred the clumps of trees and sent spirals of hot dusty air up in a mini-tornado. The Sudanese helpers drew their djellabas over their faces as their ancestors had done for hundreds of years, and the storm broke in all its fury. Doors were shut fast and shutters pulled across windows in an attempt to keep out the dust, and the wellhead was covered. Tanks of water in the square were dragged into huts or covered with wooden lids to protect them, but empty petrol drums were left to collect any rainwater that might fall, but the sky remained dull and fiery but dry.

Across the desert, the rain was falling, turning the yellow earth to dull brown and washing the sand away in eddies. 'We might be lucky and have rain, but that's miles away,' said Tony. He came out of his hut, rubbing his eyes. 'I fell asleep,' he confessed as if it was something forbidden.

'You were tired,' said Rebecca. The air held an electric charge that made her skin tingle. She tried to keep away from him, but when she turned, he was still at her back, and she wondered if he had rested with Meryl or alone. She peered out at the dusk, and the hot air was dry and harsh on her skin.

'If only it would rain!' said Sister Faith. 'But I mustn't pray for that until we know that the families in the wadi are safe.' She looked anxious. 'Hamid must be there by now, but with night falling, they'll want to stay.'

'I think we should check and take some supplies,' said Tony. The rest had restored him and he was eager for action.

'You're right, Tony,' said Sister Faith.

'Rebecca can come too,' said Tony as if doing her a favour. He glanced at her and grinned. 'You said you weren't tired, and the children like you.'

'Dr Bara said he'd go——' began Rebecca.

'You can't go with Gamel!' said Tony. 'Much too safe,' he murmured under his breath so that only she could hear. 'It wouldn't do,' he said primly. 'Besides, you can feed me as I drive.'

'What about Meryl?' Rebecca asked.

'She's too weak. Do you know, she almost fainted in my arms when I went to see her? I had to pick her up and put her to bed.' The handsome face was stern and gave away nothing. 'We leave Meryl out of this,' he said, and Rebecca knew that he wouldn't discuss anyone he loved.

'What do we take?' she asked. She was tired now and the aching in her legs from the pounding during the other journey made her want to sink into bed and sleep the clock round, but she couldn't let him see any sign of weakness or he would go on thinking her a silly, helpless female like his sister.

They loaded up the ambulance by torchlight and put food and a tent in for emergencies, with a heavy plastic sheet and a thick bundle that Sister Faith said was mosquito nets. It was strange to leave the comparative safety of the camp and Mission for the blank darkness of the desert, without even the stars to light the way, but the powerful headlights showed the dirt track clearly, and in the cab of the ambulance a compass hung to give them direction.

Once inside the vehicle, and sitting close to Tony, Rebecca lost any fear she might have had and began to enjoy the sensation of travelling, with him beside her, his arm pressed against her shoulder as he turned the wheel and a sleepy acceptance flooding her mind. She was aware of him as a man and as a sexually exciting one, but her emotions were dulled by weariness and she sensed his protectiveness again. And I haven't even got my hair loose, was her last thought before falling asleep with her head on his shoulder.

The ambulance truck bounced over a rock and she woke with a start. In the distance, the shouting grew louder and lights flared. 'Where are we?' Rebecca asked, and sat up, suddenly conscious that Tony had been driving with one arm round her, as if she belonged by his side, close with her head pressed against him.

'We're there. It isn't all that far from our camp, but these people walked, and distance makes no difference to them, once they're on the road. They plod on until they find a suitable stopping place and refuse to leave it if it has water.'

Hamid appeared out of the darkness and spoke in the local dialect. 'Speak more slowly, Hamid,' begged Tony, and listened carefully.

'What did he say?' queried Rebecca.

'He's made them move to higher ground, but some are already packing up to go back home. To them, the rains mean life and they don't think of the dangers to the children.'

'Are they all out of the wadi?' asked Rebecca.

Hamid shook his head. 'Some stay,' he said, and shrugged. He had told them to move and they refused, so what could he do?

'We must go to them and talk to them,' said Rebecca. 'Hamid, show us where they are and speak to them for us.'

Hamid climbed on to the ambulance roof and pointed. The others got back inside and went slowly over the rough ground, now shelving towards the dry river bed. The wheels dug into the loose shale and the ambulance swayed as it went lower. A few camp-fires showed the positions of the families there, and Hamid jumped off the roof and took them to the first tent.

In the distance, the wind howled, and it grew closer. A

drop of rain fell, cool and sweet, on Rebecca's face as she looked up to see the lightning, then another drop and another. Rain fell in stinging, cool sheets, drenching them all as they stood by the bank of the old river. Rebecca held out her arms to it and gulped the fresh droplets as they coursed down her face. Hamid yelled and started up the engine of the ambulance, driving it high above the river bed on to rocks as the sand dissolved and formed a morass under their feet. Long fingers of water met at the wadi, swelling the tide and washing away the earth that was so dry it was like powder, and the terrified families struggled to gather their possessions and take them to safety.

Rebecca ran down to take two babies from their mothers' arms while the women brought packs of food and clothing up the slope, and by the time they were safe, the tent had been washed away in a swirling torrent of yellow mud.

Cries came through the darkness and Hamid switched on the headlights and lit the scene, making it possible for Rebecca and Tony to help and to save as much as possible.

'No lives lost,' said Tony curtly. 'Tell them to get back further, Hamid, and to start for the Mission as soon as they can, taking the track up there. We can't drive them all, but we can fill the truck with their belongings if that helps. You drive back slowly with them, Hamid, and let the children take turns riding. You can also give Sister Faith the news that two women need our help, and we'll stay for the rest of the night and bring them in tomorrow.'

One woman had a badly bruised leg and was soon settled in the back of the ambulance. The other had blood gushing from a cut made when a piece of jagged wood was tossed towards her on the water. Rebecca dressed the wound after dusting it with sulphonamide powder as soon as it was dry and the two women were soon asleep, dry and safe and taking up all the room in the ambulance. Out in the rain, Tony pitched the tent and put down the huge sheet of plastic he had brought with him.

'Bring in the food store from the trunk and the water jar.' He laughed. 'Water enough here, but nothing to catch it in!'

Rebecca found two blankets and some cushions in the cab of the vehicle and her own holdall with a small towel and make-up, but no change of clothing.

Tony sat on the first blanket and opened up the mosquito net, while she eyed him with deep suspicion. There was only one net and if they had to lie under it they would be very cosy indeed! He hung the cord on to the tent rail and let the net hang down to the ground. Rebecca felt her wet garments clinging to her and shifted uncomfortably in the light of the lamp.

Trickles of water ran down her neck from her saturated hair and she unpinned the knot and let her hair hang down to dry, pushing it back over one shoulder after squeezing out the loose water just outside the tent flap.

The yellow lamplight played on her wet clothes and the thin dress that now clung even more seductively than the wet tee-shirt that Meryl had put on deliberately to attract Tony and Kurt, and the line of her tiny wisps of underwear showed as mere indications of another layer of fabric but did nothing to hide the lines of her thighs and breasts.

Tony stared, then turned away, rubbing his hair with the shirt he had taken off. 'Strip off,' he said, in a voice that seemed an octave deeper and had difficulty in pronouncing the words.

'I can't,' she whispered. 'I have nothing to change into.'

'You'll be chilled to the bone if you don't,' he said simply. 'Tonight will be cold and the rain will cool the earth and make it even colder. Wind chill isn't felt only in cold climates, you know.'

'I could sleep in the cab,' she ventured, but already the first joy at feeling cool had died and she shivered. With unsteady hands she unbuttoned her dress and let it fall to the ground. Tony picked it up and spread it on the plastic sheeting by the lamp with his own shirt and jeans, then came over to her and felt her still wet hair.

'Put it up again or you'll be wet all night,' he said. 'I'll squeeze out as much water as I can first.' They sat on the floor by the flap and he twisted her long hair until it was almost towel-dry, then handed her the long tress to coil again. 'At least you now smell normal,' he said. 'Gamel's Eastern promise has been washed away, and you smell of rain and river mud and . . . innocence.'

He put a hand under her chin and made her look up at him, her eyes softly hazel and full of the love she was powerless to hide. He crushed her mouth under his kiss and held her close, thigh to thigh, breast to breast, with her feet clear of the ground. A magic carpet of love, she thought faintly. No time, no ground under her, just this wonderful lightness and hunger and his arms round her pressing her ever closer, the two bodies becoming warmer and needing even more contact.

He lowered her to the blanket and sat beside her, gazing down at the cloud of fast-drying hair and caressing her arms as if they were delicate alabaster, and Rebecca was suddenly shy. A lump in her throat and a sadness that she had never felt when any man had kissed her made her turn her head away and tense her body.

'Still cold?' asked Tony tenderly, and bent to take her in his arms again.

'A pity we haven't a sauna or a jacuzzi,' she said with an attempt at lightness, then looked up at him. His expression changed. The passion in his eyes faded and his body slackened as he sat away from her.

'Forgive me,' he said. 'Oh, Becky, you have no right to look as you do and make me forget!'

Her face was a study in bewilderment. The sudden change in his manner was shattering. Just as the tent had become a haven into which she had sunk, helpless with love and longing and ready for a long night of whatever came to them, he had turned away, and certainly not because he wasn't eager for her lips, her arms and her body.

He buried his face in his hands, then looked up. 'When you look at me like that, I forget you have it all mapped out, don't you, Rebecca? You're going back to Weldon and that cheap clinic he runs. Meryl told me all about it, but you never talk of it, so I wanted to forget what she says.' He touched the line of her breast over the tiny bra and she shivered. Take me into your arms, she wanted to say, but her voice wouldn't come. 'It would be so easy to forget,' he said.

'I suppose Meryl reminded you when you . . . put her to bed today,' she said, the hurt in her heart surfacing. 'Did it never occur to you that she might be wrong? And what are you doing here with me, when she's your lover?'

His mouth tightened. 'I know Weldon means to marry you—he told me. That's the truth and you know it, so why should I doubt Meryl, who only echoes what I already knew?'

'I'm cold,' said Rebecca, and huddled down on to the blanket.

Tony wrapped her in it, swaddling her like a child, then he pulled the net down to cover her and stood away.

'Where are you going?' she asked.

He picked up the other blanket and pulled it round him tightly, hiding his taut body. 'I shall sleep in the cab.'

'The mosquitoes will get you,' said Rebecca, half dreading that he would come back, but hating her empty arms.

'Damn the mosquitoes. There's more danger in here under that net!'

She heard the cab door slam and wondered if the women in the back were awakened by it, then she snuggled down inside the blanket and tried to sleep.

The lamp flared and she hoped it wouldn't run out of gas. All alone in the tent, she felt vulnerable and lonely. Outside she heard a snuffling, grunting sound that moved round the tent and thought she heard the coughing roar of some big cat. Terrified, she sat with her knees up to her chin and the blanket over the back of her head.

Another sound, and she put her fist in her mouth to stop the scream that threatened, and her heart pounded with fear. She heard a shot, then feet running, and as the door to the tent opened, she fainted.

Moaning softly and half aware of strong arms holding her, Rebecca looked up. Tony held her close, still wrapped up in her blanket and looking at her with a cynical smile.

'Two females fainting in my arms in one day? I shall begin to think it's something I said!' he laughed, as

Rebecca glanced fearfully towards the tent flap.

'I heard wild animals,' she told him. 'I also heard a shot!' she added as she slowly recalled what had happened.

'Jackals,' he said laconically. His eyes were laughing. 'I said you shouldn't have come here. Imagine being afraid of the odd jackal!'

'They were sniffing round the tent,' she told him accusingly. Then she saw the gun he had placed outside the mosquito net. 'Did you shoot one?'

'No, I frightened them away. Some food was left by the families in the wadi and they scented it.'

'Are the women in the ambulance all right?'

'That's better,' he said. 'Yes, they're fine. They saw the gun and went back to sleep, feeling safe.'

'Don't leave me,' begged Rebecca.

'I have no intention of having you faint on me again. You're heavier than you look!' He sat cross-legged beside her under the net, like a guard in a djellaba, the rough blanket shrouding his body and taking away any indication of what was beneath it.

'You will stay?'

'When you look up, I shall be there,' he said.

Rebecca sighed and snuggled deeper into her blanket. 'Thank you,' she murmured.

'A pleasure. This isn't quite what I had in mind for tonight, but maybe it's better for telling to my grandchildren, when they ask what I did in the desert.' He lay beside her and gathered her to him, blanket and all, in a hug that was warm and brotherly. 'The rain's stopped,' he said.

Rebecca giggled. 'Any more for tennis?' she said.

CHAPTER NINE

'YOU LOOK a wreck,' said Meryl with a satisfied air.

'I'll never get the tangles out of my hair,' sighed Rebecca, 'and I'm still steaming gently as my clothes dry on me. I must get changed.'

'I put water in your hut,' said Meryl, 'and Sister Faith wants to see you as soon as you're ready, but after you've changed and eaten.'

Rebecca looked surprised. Meryl was obviously glad to see her looking wet and untidy, but she was being kind.

'Are you really better?' asked Rebecca. The other girl's face was less thin and her eyes bright.

'Fine. I had news this morning. Strange that a lot of the vans couldn't use the roads, but the one with our mail and some syringes that we badly needed managed to get through.'

'Good news?'

'I have to go back to Cairo to report to VSO and be given my next stint, probably in Kenya,' said Meryl, 'then my two years will be up and I can go home if I want that.'

'Do you want to go home?' Rebecca hung anxiously on the reply. Home for Meryl might mean London, and soon Tony would be going back too.

'It depends,' said Meryl. 'Kurt wants to do a Kenya safari before he goes back to the States, and we might team up after I've finished work.' She glanced at Rebecca. 'We got to know each other better when we were ill, and we have a lot in common.'

'I thought you and Tony . . .'

'So did I! I tried my best, but have you ever had the sensation that you take one step forward and two steps back in this everlasting sand? I thought he'd fall for me out here, with so little competition, but here I am, slipping back in the sand and having to admit I can't have him.' Meryl spoke frankly and with a certain grim humour. 'The wretched man was brought up in a family of sisters who sound like men to me! They never get the same mystic feeling about women unless they're the helpless type like the other sister who died.'

'He's probably seen girls in every stage of development and dress and will marry someone like them,' agreed Rebecca.

'He's all male,' mused Meryl. 'I still lust after him, but I can cut my losses. Tell me, just for the record, did he make love to you last night?' Her eyes were hard and the glitter might have been unshed tears.

'He chased jackals and left me under the mosquito net,' Rebecca told her simply.

'Thank you for that. If even you couldn't manage it, then I don't feel so bad.'

'Do you mean he isn't in love with you, Meryl?'

''Fraid not. I tried to warn you off, but there was no need. He thinks I'm a bit too . . . obvious. Kurt doesn't mind my way-out clothes and behaviour and he might even learn to love me, among all those zebras and lions. Nothing like the great outdoors to bring out the macho male in him.' Meryl winked. 'I might not see you again. Good luck with your clinic and that dishy-sounding man in London.'

'London?' It seemed far away now and Rebecca could not visualise herself walking once more down Park Lane or feeding the ducks in St James's Park, and Beattie's, her beloved training school, was a memory. 'I go back soon, but I have no idea what I shall do,' she said.

'Tony said you'll be married as soon as you get back and that you're here just to have a last look at freedom. You must be marrying a nice guy,' Meryl went on enviously. 'I can't see any man I know letting a girl go so easily, and on his suggestion too.' She sighed. 'He must trust you more than is good for him, the poor fool, or does it bring out the loyal little-woman syndrome with you? No wonder you screw that lovely hair up so tight and wear awful hats!'

She eyed the now knotty hair and laughed. 'I'd cut it off and start again. You might get it combed out, but it will take days to really make it smooth again. All you need now is a few lice in it and you'll be in real trouble,' she added.

'Lice?' Rebecca looked horrified.

'Of course. They're everywhere. Some of the last batch of kids were crawling!'

Rebecca forgot she ought to put the record straight and convince Meryl that Paul had not encouraged her to come to Africa, but had objected strongly and that they had quarrelled and parted. *'Lice?'* she said again, and imagined her hair felt odd and her scalp itched.

'I'll take a look if you like,' said Meryl with a burst of generosity. 'Get some food and see Sister Faith, and I'll be here with nit comb and brush and a de-lousing lotion if you need it, but it won't smell very nice.'

'I may not have them,' said Rebecca hopefully.

'Of course you haven't!' Meryl was laughing. 'You'd have felt them by now, but I will have a look and you could do the same for me. It's wise to check when we deal with so many people here.'

The dining table bore signs of a recent meal and Rebecca sat at one end that she cleared of used dishes. A Sudanese cook brought her fresh bread and jam and coffee and a dish of mangoes. She sipped the hot coffee and felt refreshed, and wondered why hot drinks were still the most welcome even in the heat of Africa. Now, the air was clear and the rain had gone, leaving the sand clean and already showing signs of green as dormant shoots absorbed the water. Her skin was cool and she could move freely without the heat pressing down on her, but her emotions were drained.

Paul had really made it his business to show that she was his property, she thought bitterly; so even if another man fell in love with her, he would hold back if he was an honourable man. Love? She gave a tired smile. Paul loved her for his own ends and Tony wanted her as a man wants something to possess when his passion is roused, with a fleeting need, a transient, thrusting, animal urge to proclaim his sexuality. That was not love as she felt it, this vibrant yearning, this tender need to touch and be close, this sensation of falling through eternity when he held her in his arms.

'Sister Faith is waiting, if you have a minute,' said Meryl from the door.

Rebecca started. She had lingered over the food and dreamed of the impossible. She almost ran to the hut where Sister Faith was feeding babies.

'I'm sorry, Sister—I didn't know you wanted me urgently.'

'Nor did I,' said the nun, and smiled. 'In fact, we have less to do now than at any time during the past five months. Come and sit here and feed this one, and we can talk.' She handed over a tiny brown body that was fairly plump and showed no signs of dysentery. 'Remember her? She was one you had to force-feed and the mother took her away to the wadi before she was really fit, but she's doing well. If we can get some protein into her before they start the trek back to Ethiopia, she may survive.'

The tiny mouth opened and shut obediently as the food went in, and the baby snuggled up to Rebecca and fell asleep as soon as the last spoonful was taken. Rebecca smoothed the tight black curls and handed the child back to her mother. Something stirred in the hair and she saw a headlouse escaping into the curls.

'Now, I wanted to see you, Becky.' Sister patted the back of the baby she held and waited for the burp before putting her in the padded box that served as a cot until the mother came for her. 'There's a great exodus today from all the camps this side of the border. The police will be overwhelmed and I can see them letting hundreds through without visas or papers of any kind.' She smiled. 'That at least is not our business. With luck and God's grace, we may now be able to revert to what we should be, a mission and hospital on a small scale for the benefit of local people and travellers.'

'But is that possible?' asked Rebecca. 'What if the rains haven't been enough?'

'They'll give one harvest and perhaps two, and then there could be a few years of sufficient rain. Remember your Bible? The seven lean years and the seven good years? It does happen out here, even if not quite like that. Feast and famine is common in all hot countries where the desert creeps in and robs the soil until the rains come.'

Rebecca watched the sweet face and wondered why she was telling her this, then it dawned on her that she might not be needed. 'Are you hinting that you want me to go?' she said in a low voice, and was shaken by the pain it caused her to think she would be leaving.

'Not at once, Becky. What I want you to do is to go to Khartoum with the next truck, as we badly need supplies. The crowds passing through here have been our own personal plague of locusts, and however much we bless the good Lord for making it possible to help them, they've left us with so little that unless we have supplies from Khartoum, we shall have to close down the clinic.'

'Meryl's going to Cairo, Sister. She could send supplies back to you on her way.'

Sister Faith shook her head. 'Meryl will go by train from Gedaref, as they want her there as soon as possible.'

'Kurt? Will he be going too?' asked Rebecca.

'He leaves in a week's time, as soon as he's helped me to clear one of the old huts and make it habitable. It's time he left. He's been useful and has used Africa to sort out his soul.' Sister Faith smiled. 'Not everyone comes to the same conclusion, and his needs are worldly, but now he does know what he wants, and that's a kind of victory.'

'When do you want me to go?' Rebecca dared not ask if she would go with one of the nuns or with Tony. Hamid might even be sent to drive the truck with her.

'Dr Bara will drive one truck and Tony the Range Rover, but Hamid will go too, to drive the Range Rover back here.'

Rebecca stared at her. 'So Tony doesn't come back?'

'No, he'll go to Cairo to an international congress held next month, and he needs to meet a lot of people first.'

'Meryl's going to Cairo,' said Rebecca.

'But not with Tony,' the gentle voice said with surprising firmness, and when Rebecca looked at her, she saw that Sister Faith knew far more about the members of her staff than at first appeared. 'Meryl will meet Kurt later, and I think they'll marry,' she added.

'So how long do I stay here after the visit to Khartoum, Sister?'

'As long as you like, Becky, but I advise a short holiday away from all tensions before you start anything new.'

'Tony thinks I'm going back to a health farm in England,' said Rebecca.

'But your heart tells you this is not what you want, doesn't it? That's why you must take time to think, and please don't rush back to Dr Weldon.'

'I'd forgotten—you met Paul, Sister.' Rebecca spoke eagerly. 'He loves me and wants me to marry him, and he can make life quite interesting.' The opinion of this calm unworldly woman was essential now.

'Take time to think, and go and speak to the Pyramids. They are built to other gods but they have the wisdom of the ages. They have peace,' the nun added simply, and took another child from its mother's arms.

Rebecca left the hut and walked back to find Meryl. Her bags were packed ready for the truck to take her to Gedaref, but she had to wait for another hour before leaving, so she examined Rebecca's scalp and tried to comb out the worst of the tangles. 'It's no use,' she said at last. 'We have plenty of water now, so why not wash it and brush it out when it's wet? No nits,' she announced airily, and handed the comb to Rebecca.

It was strange to be gently combing the hair of a woman she had no cause to like, but Rebecca did so, and envied the ease of care that short hair gave. Her own now hung at her back ready for the much-needed shampoo, and it felt heavy and lacklustre. 'No lice,' she said at last, and they both laughed. 'I itched all over as soon as you mentioned them, and the next baby I fed was covered with them,' said Rebecca.

'Wave me off, Becky,' said Meryl. 'I hate leaving anywhere that's been my home for even a month, and I've been here for ages, off and on,' and when the truck lurched over the muddy track, with Kurt and Sister Faith and Rebecca waving, Meryl was in tears.

Kurt walked back with Rebecca. 'She's got guts, and a type of body that makes me want to take out a lease on her,' he admitted. He breathed deeply. 'I'm going to miss her.'

'But not for long,' suggested Rebecca.

'No, you're darned right. Not for long. I'll finish here and get out for good. It's back home for me in about two months from now, and she's coming with me.'

Rebecca sterilised all the syringes and needles, throwing out any needles that were blunted but being careful over the selection as needles were in short supply. She wondered what the Sister in the diabetic wing at Beattie's would think of such old-fashioned equipment, and contrasted the tray of glass and metal syringes that could be used time after time after time, with the packs of disposables that were tossed into the bin after being used once.

'It pays to have them in reserve wherever you are,' said Sister Faith. 'If a catastrophe happened, anywhere, a few of these would be useful while supplies came, and if we're very careful with sterilising, we have no increase in hepatitis or any of the other transmittable diseases.'

'I shall value equipment far more in future,' said Rebecca, and tried not to think of the waste there would be in a place like the Hawthorne where the need to impress the rich clientele would make new equipment a priority at all times.

At the evening meal, taken late after the last of the travellers had gone, Kurt was silent and almost morose. Tony came in even later and sank down as if weary and ate without contributing much to the conversation. Rebecca glanced at the two stony faces and her heart sank. They missed Meryl far more than either of them had thought possible. She finished her meal and made her excuses, saying she needed a good night before starting out in the morning.

Once more she had the hut to herself, and she didn't bother to see if Hamid was by her door, but slept until dawn and the fresh air through the mosquito netting on the window roused her.

A buzz of activity filled the courtyard, and she washed hurriedly and coiled her now clean hair into a neat plait over her head. If they stayed the night in Khartoum, she would need a change of clothing and some personal items. She hurried over to breakfast and found the men there eating. Dr Bara greeted her with a smile and the others nodded. It looked as if they were going to have a very subdued journey, and Rebecca wasn't looking forward to travelling with two men who had thoughts only for the girl who had just left.

If you'd stayed a little longer, Meryl, you might have made Tony, she thought. He seemed to avoid any contact with her, and slipped away to finish loading the truck with empty gas bottles, boxes for supplies and his own bags.

Her mouth was dry as she sat beside him in the Range

Rover. His bags were stacked up behind them and she knew that everything he had brought to the camp was leaving with him. I may never see you again, she thought, and here you are, sitting beside me as if you were made of stone, or like one of the statues gazing forever over the desert with no thought of the people walking beneath it.

'I'm here,' she whispered to herself under the roar of the engine. 'I'm here and alive and I love you, and yet you avoid touching my hand, and you're already in Cairo in your mind.'

'What did you say?' asked Tony.

'Nothing. Just thinking out loud,' she replied.

'Not such a hot journey as last time,' he said politely. 'By the way, there was some mail for you this morning, and some for me. It came on the truck that collected Meryl.' He nodded towards the glove tray. 'Must be anxious about you—three from the same place with the same handwriting.'

Rebecca took one without looking at the date and opened it. Recognising Paul's exuberant handwriting.

'Aren't you going to open the first one first? Don't you want to savour every word in sequence to make up for the delay they had in reaching you?' The voice was hard and tinged with sarcasm.

'This will do,' she said coldly, and read the first few lines. It was a long letter, but it said little more than come home soon, don't be a fool, I want to marry you as soon as you get back, and the clinic needs you. There were snippets of news about friends at Beattie's, but mostly friends of Paul's with whom she had very little in common.

She flipped through the pages of all the letters and found them much the same as the first, but written at

intervals of five days. She thrust them back into the
envelopes and put them in her holdall.

'That was quick. I thought you'd be reading them
when we reached Khartoum,' Tony remarked.

'I never read in cars. It makes me feel sick,' said
Rebecca, but she didn't add that her present nausea had
nothing to do with the motion of the vehicle. Paul
seemed with them in the cab, smooth and insistent,
making her feel trapped. If I go back now, I shall be
unable to stop his plans, she thought. He'll crush any
objections I have and make himself so pleasant that I
shall be helpless, with no real excuse against marrying
him and taking up my place in the Spa. She glanced at
the stern profile beside her and wanted to shake him into
some kind of feeling, even if that feeling was anger and
not love.

'The constant lover,' said Tony. 'You'll be able to sink
into a cosy nest and never have to face the rough desert
again.'

'I might not marry him,' she ventured.

'Come now, he told me of your plans, and those letters
prove that he's very anxious to see you again. Of course
when you get back, you'll know how much you've
missed him. I told you you should never have come here,
Becky.' There was pain in the voice, and he had used her
pet name.

'I wanted to come, and I may stay on,' she said
defiantly.

'Sister Faith has all the staff she needs in less troubled
times. The new team will be here next month and will
take over when you come to Khartoum again.' Tony
glanced at her for the first time. 'There are rumours that
a light aircraft might be available to take you to Cairo, if
there's no room in the truck. When the next team come,

they'll need only the truck to bring them back, leaving only enough room for one driver who would have to return with them.'

'She's told you I'm to leave?'

'She thinks it best for you,' he said.

'I've proved that I can stand the heat and the work load,' Rebecca said defiantly.

'I admit it. You've amazed me in so many ways, and I wish . . .'

'What do you wish, Tony?'

'I wish I'd taken you more seriously at the beginning and realised what you're like,' he said softly.

'But you thought I was a silly little girl with long hair and not a thought in my head!' she retorted vehemently.

'I thought you too fragile and lovely for such work,' he corrected.

'Sister Faith suggested that I take a holiday on my way back. She wants me to visit Cario while I'm here.' Rebecca looked ahead. If he says nothing, I shall know he wants to see the back of me for ever, she thought, and I shall fly straight back to London and Paul. I shall stay in Cairo for one night and see the Pyramids, and then leave Africa for ever.

'You shouldn't miss the Pyramids,' he agreed, but made no reference to his own stay during the congress, and talked about Cario Museum.

'I might sign on with VSO and not go home,' she said cautiously.

'Too long a commitment,' he said firmly. 'You'd never make it.' He went red. 'Sorry—it's a habit. One of my sisters went to Zaire and had a nasty attack of malaria and was ill for a long time.'

'Not one of your Amazonian sisters? Surely it must have been the little girl who died?' Rebecca knew she sounded unfeeling, but she had ceased to care.

'It was one of my elder sisters, who'd never been ill,' he admitted. 'Not my stepsister Michelle.'

'Your *stepsister*?' Tony nodded. 'I'm sorry—I had no idea.' So Michelle was different, and not related by blood. It was a relief in a way to know that Tony had been half in love with someone who wasn't a blood relative, someone with long hair that made her look childlike and so even more attractive among so many healthy females who had grown up with him.

'My father married a widow with one child, Michelle, who lived with us for a short while, travelled on a scholarship and died in India,' he said simply.

Then Dr Bara called to them to stop for a rest, and they sat under the awning that had once almost led to a night of love, and somehow, after the food was packed away again, Rebecca found herself in the cab with Dr Bara while Hamid took her place in the Range Rover.

Dr Bara talked of the Mission and the work he hoped to do with new drugs for the treatment of obscure tropical diseases, while Rebecca sat in the jolting vehicle, trying to appear interested, but she wanted to ask him to stop and let Tony come back beside her. It wasn't just because she longed for the physical contact of the man she knew she loved as she could never love another human being, but Gamel Bara drove at such a speed over rough ground that she thought she might be shot out through the roof at any minute.

They arrived in a cloud of dust outside the hotel in Khartoum, where they managed to find rooms as the pressure on accommodation had eased, and Rebecca luxuriated under the first shower she had had for days. It was wonderful to cover her body with sweet-smelling soap from her precious supply and to dry and powder herself and to feel clean and civilised. I'd miss the good things of life if I had to do without them for ever, she thought with a trace of guilt. So many people had to do without and had never known such luxury as clean water and fresh towels.

In her bag, she found the oil that Dr Bara had given her and applied it cautiously, half afraid it might suddenly burst into the perfume that the other bottle contained, but it made her hair feel good, smelled mild and interesting, but not oppressive, and she emerged for dinner slightly freckled and brown but glowing with health and beauty. Her clean dress was of emerald green cotton that made her skin look good and her eyes take on a hint of the green.

Almost defiantly, she took the pins from her bound hair and let it fall loose. He's going away tomorrow and I may never see him alone again, she told herself. He *shall* remember me, even if he wants to forget that once he held me in his arms and his body longed for mine, his mouth possessed my lips, my heart and my soul. I must make him take away something of me, if only a memory tied up with his love for Michelle.

Her hair flowed smoothly over her shoulders as she walked into the dining room. The air stirred by the vast overhead fans found tendrils that wouldn't obey brush or comb and she felt it drifting on her shoulders.

Tony stood up as she came into the room and stared. His hand held a glass in his hand that snapped off at the stem as his hand crushed it and he had to dry his hand and the table top with a paper napkin. Rebecca sat opposite him with Dr Bara between them on one side and another Sudanese doctor who had come to see Bara on the other. With a smile, she accepted a glass of

Kirkady from Dr Bara and sipped it, watching the faces
of the men talking.

From time to time, Tony looked at her without smiling. He talked about London to satisfy the curiosity of
the other Sudanese doctor who had never been there,
and Gamel Bara mentioned people and places he had
seen in England and Scotland. A formal dinner party
among strangers couldn't have felt more detached, more
remote from Rebecca's usual warm contacts with
friends, and she begged to be excused for the night.
Tony stood up as she left, but she waved away his offer to
escort her to her room, and saw the approval in the eyes
of the Sudanese.

Bitterly, as she undressed, she wondered if they could
ever guess that she had not left alone out of modesty, but
out of fear of what would happen if Tony touched her
again, kissed her, even in friendship, or took her in his
arms. One touch of love would break down any resolve
she had of letting him go, and she knew that a deep and
guilty passion raged under those dark eyes that could be
released in a torrent more destroying than the rains of
Africa. 'Why does he still love Michelle? Why can't he
see that I don't love Paul?' she muttered. She slipped
between clean sheets and even that bliss couldn't heal
the smarting wounds that his dark glances caused.

She tossed in bed. Meryl had admitted that she had
made no headway with him, Michelle was dead and
gone, leaving just a sentimental memory of a girl with
long bright hair, and Paul was far away. Sounds from a
street vender, still selling food at this late hour, and the
soft throb of music and drums made Rebecca's flesh
soften, her thighs limp with longing and her lips parted,
waiting for the healing touch of love, but she heard a
door slam, the sounds faded and she had no release.

She turned over and shut her eyes, only to dream of being overtaken by the river in flood, water clutching at her ankles and soft mud trying to take her down into the wadi. A bright light was before her—bringing help or more danger? She shuddered, and woke to find the sun streaming through the meshed windows on to her face.

A tray of fruit juice and bread and jam appeared as soon as she was dressed and ready for breakfast. She looked at the girl who brought it. 'The doctor said you eat here, miss,' she said firmly. 'Rest before going back.' She smiled, showing white teeth against brown skin.

Rebecca sank on to the bed again and sipped fresh orange juice. So he didn't want to see her. She ate almost mechanically, disciplined to eat by her time at the Mission, but the food could have been dry sand and the fresh drinks like the brackish water from the well. Pride made her stay in her room until a tap on the door followed by Dr Bara's voice asked her to come to the front of the hotel.

Tony was strapping up one of his bags. He looked up at her and resumed what he was doing. Dr Bara said, 'Tony has to leave now, Sister Becky, and we leave in half an hour. I hope you are rested.'

'I suppose this is goodbye,' faltered Rebecca, unable to meet the anger in the dark eyes of a man who had sometimes smiled at her, sometimes looked at her with love.

'So you did bother to come out of your room in time to say that?' The voice was the one she hated, full of anger and repressed pride.

'You sent a message that I must breakfast in my room and rest,' she said.

'That was Bara.' His expression softened. 'I'm sorry, I thought you were avoiding me.' He took her hand in his, as anyone would who was going away and had to make formal goodbyes, but he held it tight, and once more, the vital sensation of them being linked by an intangible thread of sexuality made her eyes blur and her lips to quiver.

'Goodbye, Becky,' he said. 'Oh, God, I wanted to say so much, but Gamel is right. You're going to be married and I have no right to touch you.'

'I'm not going to marry Paul,' Rebecca said firmly. 'I know what he told you and what you think I've promised but I shall never marry him.' Her voice was low, and Tony bent to hear better.

'What did you say? Damned camels! Can't hear a word.'

The train of camels passed the hotel, and the loud cries of the camel drivers and the moans of the beasts faded. A car horn sounded and repeated its call. 'You must leave now, Tony. Hamid has loaded your bags,' said Dr Bara.

Rebecca looked up into the face that was etched on her heart for ever, while Dr Bara looked on, smiling. Tony kissed her on both cheeks in the formal French way and turned away. At the door of the taxi, he turned and said something, but once again the intolerable noise of traffic drowned his words. She thought he said, 'See you by the Pyramids,' but she knew this was self-delusion.

'Goodbye, my love,' she breathed, then ran back into the hotel, to sit on the bed with clenched hands and dry, hot eyes until she could breathe normally, smile with a feeling of breaking glass behind it, and pack her bag for the journey back to the Mission.

'Ready,' she said firmly as Dr Bara put her bag behind her seat. 'Who drives?' she asked, with a degree of apprehension.

'I shall drive you, and Hamid must find room to drive the truck. We have so many supplies that both vehicles are full and we shall have to go more slowly,' said Dr Bara in an aggrieved voice. 'We shall take an extra hour.'

'I don't mind,' said Rebecca. 'Go as slowly as you like.' She settled back, and at first Dr Bara drove well and carefully, as the heavily-laden Range Rover ploughed through wet sand and dry rubble. The air was hot again as the sun rose and the ground had given up its excess water since the rains.

'We shall miss you all,' said Dr Bara, after a few miles of silence. 'Even Meryl will be missed, as she was good at her work. Anthony will stay in Cairo for a few weeks for the congress and to see Egypt and write up some of this notes about cases here.'

'Kurt is going too,' said Rebecca, 'and soon I must go back myself.'

'To take up married life,' said Bara with satisfaction.

'No, I shan't marry Paul,' she said. Even if Tony was too deaf or preoccupied to hear her, she must let it be known. 'Paul wants me to marry him, but I've never said I would. I have no intention of working with him either. I might sign up for VSO if they'll have me, but Sister Faith thinks I ought to have a holiday first.'

The steering wheel slipped and the car nearly hit a stunted bush. Dr Bara gave a low whistle of annoyance.

'Now you tell me!' he exclaimed, and she had to glance at him sharply to believe he was not a true Scot.

'Meryl told me that she and Tony were . . . would be . . .' she began.

'And he was told you would marry that doctor in London.' Dr Bara laughed aloud. 'I shall never understand you Brits,' he said. 'We arrange things better here.

There's never any doubt who a woman marries.'

'It's good to be able to choose,' replied Rebecca. 'At least I can't be forced into marrying Paul.'

'And you want a man of your own choosing? A man who at this moment will be arriving alone at the Hyatt Hotel in Cairo?' Dr Bara shook his head.

'I tried to tell him,' said Rebecca. 'It's no use; he may not be in love with Meryl, but he does carry a memory of a stepsister who died, and he thinks of me as he did her, that I'm fragile, and far too much like her to give him peace of mind. She too had hair like mine.'

'Love? That is something that we don't think so important here. We make good marriages and the women bear children and keep house, and if they are poor, they work in the fields, but there's affection and friendship and partnership.'

'But women aren't considered when sex is concerned,' Rebecca said.

'No, that is something I fight,' said Gamel. 'I am to marry a girl who is finishing her course at London University, and she was brought up by enlightened parents who did not have her circumcised as a child.'

'I'm glad,' said Rebecca. 'I hope you'll be very happy together, and when you come to London to see her you must introduce me.'

They drove on across the ravaged earth, in and out of deep potholes and over shallow streams. 'We're nearly there,' said Dr Bara, in a consoling voice. 'Not much longer now, and you shall rest and eat and talk to Sister Faith.'

The camp lay over the next rise, and yet the going had never been so rough. One minute the Range Rover was going smoothly and the way seemed clear, and the next, the ground opened before them where the soil was washed away. The vehicle slewed to the right and tipped half over, throwing boxes and cases off balance. The seat-belt prevented Rebecca from falling out, but a box with a rigid edge shifted and struck her head.

Dimly she heard Dr Bara shout to Hamid to drive quickly to the Mission and fetch the ambulance, then there was darkness, shot with stabbing colours and pain, and oblivion.

CHAPTER TEN

'STAY FLAT,' said a voice, and a hand rested on her shoulder as Rebecca made an effort to sit up. She obeyed thankfully, as points of light from a lamp overhead made her head throb and she could hear her own pulse beating somewhere deep inside her head.

'No fracture—I'm almost sure of that. Maybe a small crack, but no need for surgery.' The voice was Scottish and reassuring. 'Rest and some tidying-up of the wound and she'll be as right as rain soon, apart from an appalling headache.'

'Thank God,' said Sister Faith. The voices trailed away, but Rebecca heard Dr Bara say, when Sister Faith tried to console him,

'I blame myself for not seeing the ground had shifted. I should have avoided it.'

Rebecca forced her mind back to the journey in the Range Rover. She recalled the drive, hair-raising as usual when Gamel Bara drove the vehicle, but she had no recollection of a crash. She dismissed all thought as too tiring and spent the next day sleeping, drinking the liquid held to her lips and being washed by the caring hands of the nuns.

Night came and went, once or twice, she couldn't remember, and once her head hurt as icy local anaesthetic spray was applied to her head wound and she felt pressure rather than pain and a trickle of fluid was mopped up from her cheek that could have been blood or warm water.

'Once the hair grows again it will never be noticed,' said Sister Faith, and Rebecca heard the sound of metal instruments on glass as Dr Bara finished re-stitching a part of the scar.

'What happened?' she asked weakly, several times, but either the soft-moving Sudanese girl didn't understand, or she had been told to keep the patient quiet.

'What happened?' she demanded one morning when Sister Faith came in and found her sitting up in bed for the first time, with a feeling that maybe her head was still there and not so painful.

'A box in the truck fell and hurt you,' said Sister Faith. Rebecca nodded. It must have been a very big box, she thought.

'May I get up?' she asked. 'How long have I been here?'

'You may get up this evening when it's cooler, and you've been here for four days.' Sister Faith called for a girl to fetch Dr Bara. 'We must make an examination before you get up,' she said, and within minutes Rebecca was once again flat on the bed, with Dr Bara peering into her eyes with an ophthalmoscope, examining her ears with an auroscope and putting her through all the normal movements that the human neck can make.

'Fine,' he said at last. 'A few bruises and cuts, and those stitches must come out in a few days' time, but there's nothing lasting. Even your hair will grow back.' He looked down at her and she saw that he was uneasy.

'Are you sure I'm all right?' she asked anxiously. 'You don't look very happy about me.'

'It's your hair,' he mumbled. 'I'm truly sorry, Sister Becky, but there was so much blood that we had to cut a lot of it away from the torn skin.'

Rebecca put a hand up to what had been a swathe of

bandages before this examination and felt the long hair on one side of her head. It was loose and clean and as she remembered it. She gently felt for the line of the wound, now sealed in Collodion syrup. The area of skin round the wound was covered with a fine growth of hair like a one-day beard.

'We had to shave the head round the wound before applying Collodion in case of infection in the hair follicles,' Dr Bara explained. 'It will grow again. I'm verra, verra sorry.'

'You mustn't blame yourself,' said Rebecca. 'I couldn't have driven that car for more than a hundred yards in those conditions. It was an accident.'

'I was driving,' he said firmly. 'It was my fault, and I must try to make up for it.'

'You have,' she said, and touched his hand. 'You've given me every possible care, and after a holiday I shall be fine.'

'A holiday?' His smile was white and triumphant. 'That is easy.' He swept away, leaving Rebecca wondering if he had gone mad.

'Dr Bara is going to arrange a plane to take you to Cairo, Becky,' said Sister Faith later. 'That's not new as we thought it convenient, and there'll be one here next week, bringing a local dignitary back to his town.' Sister Faith folded a towel and put it on the wooden stand by the bed, then she took one end of the sheet on the bed while Rebecca took the other and together they straightened it. 'How does it feel to be up?'

'Wonderful! I've nothing more than a headache now, but not bad enough to need pain-killers any more.'

Sister Faith sat on the bed. 'Some Sudanese are quite wealthy,' she said. 'Many people in Europe think they should help their own people more if they have money, but it isn't as easy as that. Politics come into it, and local customs, and as you've seen, a mass of people suddenly appearing here takes far more than money. It needs care and personal attention, with supplies brought in at considerable expense in time and resources.'

'Why tell me this, Sister Faith? I know it all.'

'Dr Bara comes from a wealthy family, and besides his work here and in his researches against diseases in his own country, he gives us most of the money we need for the day-to-day running of the camp.' Rebecca's eyes widened. 'So, if he offers you a holiday, please take it and save his pride. He feels so guilty about your accident that you'll be doing him a great service if you accept what he has in mind for you.'

'What's that?' asked Rebecca.'

'He's booked a room for you in Cairo and tours to take you to see the ancient remains,' Sister Faith went on.

'But I can't accept that! It costs a bomb to stay anywhere pleasant in such a place!'

'Please, Becky. It's hard to accept goodness and so easy to give it. You know that and so do I. Accept and go soon, and take time to sort out your mind.'

'Have you a mirror, Sister?'

'I wondered when you'd ask for that. Here you are. I'm afraid your hair is ruined for a while, but a hat will hide most of it.'

Rebecca couldn't decide if she wanted to laugh or cry. 'I feel like Janus, the two-faced god! This way I'm normal, and this way I'm a skinhead!'

She propped up the mirror and examined herself. The scissors were sharp and easily handled, and she took a long tress of hair and snipped it off just below her ear. At once the balance was better, and she continued until a heap of bright hair lay in a rejected coil and her head felt

oddly light. For half an hour she trimmed and cut and
gently combed the short style she had evolved, then she
smiled. 'Hello, Becky,' she said. The short hair curled
more without the weight of the old style and the fine fuzz
made a veil over the scar.

By the next day she was walking about and helping
Sister Faith to mix feeds. In two days she was used to her
hair and enjoyed the freedom it gave her, and in another
five days the scar was barely visible except at close range
as the neighbouring hair fluffed up round it.

'You are doing me a favour,' said Dr Bara when she
tried to thank him for his offer. 'I shall come with you to
make sure that you have everything you need. I shall fly
back here after meeting people at the congress, and
you'll have lots of time to see Egypt before you go
home.'

'You're going to the congress? I thought it was over.'
Rebecca's heart beat faster. If it was not over yet, then
Tony had not left Egypt.

'The last day, and I shall meet all the people I want to
see, and find a few old friends. I shall take you to the
dinner on the last night and put you in touch with people
who can help you if you need someone while you are in
Cairo.'

'Oh, thank you! I dreaded the thought of going there
alone, but once there, I know I shall enjoy it.'

'With so much water stored and the well full, you can
wash all your clothes and have them ready for Cairo,'
said Sister Faith. She seemed to be taking a great interest
in her holiday, and Rebecca teased her and said she was
glad to be rid of her, but the nun only smiled and said,
'You'll come back one day to see us. They say that once
you've smelled Africa, you must return.' She hurried
away and came back with a pale blue garment over her

arm. 'Take this with you. I know you haven't dresses for evening and I have such unsuitable things given to me by grateful patients. Please take it.'

Rebecca held out the silk djellaba against her front and gasped. 'It's exquisite, Sister!'

'Take it and wear it, and don't thank me. I have so little but service to give that this is a real blessing for me.'

Carefully the garment was packed, and the last irridescent butterfly embroidered on it disappeared into the bag, and Dr Bara was ready to leave in the repaired Range Rover, driven sedately by Hamid, to the small airstrip outside Gedaref, and the figures of the white-robed nuns and Sudanese became dots on the landscape.

Rebecca wiped her eyes. 'I shall miss them,' she said.

'You may come back if your work brings you,' said Dr Bara. He was dressed in Western clothes and looked unfamiliar. His smart briefcase and well-cut suit showed him to be wealthy and important, and when they reached the airport he was treated with respect. Rebecca thought of the lovely djellaba in her bag and sighed with relief. If he was going to take her to dinner, she would need more than cotton dresses or jeans and safari boots.

Cairo lay sprawling beneath them, mile after mile of crowded streets huddled by the river, and beyond, the desert. 'Look there.' Dr Bara pointed and Rebecca saw the Pyramids for the first time. From the air they looked small until she saw the tiny trail of camels on a ridge close by, and it put them into perspective.

The car that waited for them was polished and almost new. Until that moment, Rebecca had had no idea where they were going, but Dr Bara turned to her and said, 'I think you'll enjoy the Hyatt. It's one of the big hotels where you will meet many tourists and people from the UK. A lot of them will be on your tours and you'll feel safe.'

'The Hyatt? I've heard of it,' she began.

'Of course. Tony Brent is staying there, but I didn't mention it to you as I thought you might object to meeting him again.' His smile was broad and he was teasing her. 'Brace yourself, my lass, you'll need all your wits.' He chuckled. 'A wee bairn with shorn hair. Just wait! He's the one for a shock.'

Rebecca blushed, knowing that if she had been given any choice, she would have fled, and taken the first plane home, but the marble entrance of the hotel opened up before them and she was signing in and taking the keys to her room. 'I have a meeting but will pick you up here in the foyer at eight this evening,' Dr Bara told her, 'so can you amuse yourself for a few hours?'

She glanced at the row of smart shops in the hotel and the air-conditioned lounges, and her eyes sparkled. 'It's wonderful,' she smiled.

After settling in her room and resisting the temptation to sink into a warm bath, she wandered down to the shops. There were sandals of every kind from flat leather ones to exotic ones that could only have been made in such a city. She fitted on a pair of white ones with tiny stars of pale blue on the straps and the high heels. This was another world. She asked for coffee and was served with it quickly and offered the choice of the gâteau trolley, but she was too excited to eat. Only another hour before she must be ready, so she bathed and changed, brushing her hair with care as the scar was still sore, and finding it dry.

In her toilet bag she found, not the cream conditioner she expected, but the small phial of oil that Dr Bara had given her by mistake. She took a tiny amount on the tip

of one finger and applied it to the dry skin and felt it
relax. The scent was wonderful, but in such a small
quantity not overpowering. It went with the flowing robe
that fitted over her shoulders and softly outlined her
body as she moved.

A tap on the door made her start, but she called,
'Come in,' and turned to see if Dr Bara was in evening
dress.

'What the hell have you done to your hair?' asked
Tony.

'Didn't Dr Bara tell you?' she said weakly.

'He told me you had an accident but were better.'

He stood in the open doorway dressed in a light linen
suit with a vivid tie of blues and rusts and green. His hair
was shining and he looked as if he had never worked in a
refugee camp or handled anything more dirty than a
shoe brush.

'Where's Dr Bara?' asked Rebecca.

'He asked me to collect you,' said Tony. He seemed ill
at ease and glanced at his watch. 'We must go, if you're
ready. I have a car waiting.'

Rebecca picked up the small purse she had bought to
match the sandals and followed him to the elevator. It
was already quite full when the doors opened to take
them down and she was aware of Tony staring at her as if
he was shocked. She moved restlessly. I thought I
looked rather good, she thought, and hated her new
hairstyle for the first time.

The dinner was lengthy and varied, but Rebecca ate
but tasted nothing, drank and couldn't say what was in
her glass. Dr Bara and Tony talked over her head and
discussed people she had never met and places of which
she had only heard. The speeches too were intermin-
able, and her head ached. She longed for solitude and

for the evening to end. She was far more lonely sitting in the crowded room than if she had been locked in her bedroom.

'Your head aches?' asked Dr Bara, at last.

'Would you excuse me if I left?' she asked in a low voice.

'See you tomorrow before I leave,' he whispered, and handed the car keys to Tony. 'Take her for some air—and don't drive fast,' he added with the air of a careful driver.

'I don't want to take you away,' Rebecca said in a sudden panic.

'Get up quietly and follow me out,' was all Tony said, and in another minute she was sitting in the limousine, being driven through the congested streets of Cairo and out into the desert.

'Where are we going?' she asked.

'I told you I'd meet you by the Pyramids,' he said.

He drove on until the noise of the city was far behind them and the immense shapes of the ancient Pyramids loomed up against a sky full of stars and a moon that cast mysterious shadows as it had done for so many thousands of years.

They walked by the edge of the sand and sat on the wall where by day the camel drivers waited with their animals. The night air was cool, and Rebecca shivered, but not with chill.

'What did you do with your hair?' asked Tony, and his hand reached out to touch the light curls.

'I burned them. They were the past, and I shall never grow it long again.'

'No more lovely long hair,' he said ruefully.

'It's dead, as Michelle is dead,' she said softly.

'And this is the place of all truth,' he said. His arms

were round her, gently, his face close to hers. 'You're not going back to Weldon—Gamel told me.'

'I might——' Rebecca began.

'The truth,' said Tony, and kissed her. 'Can you go back now, having been here with me?' His arms enfolded her, and she rested her head against him while her body answered his question. She melted like the bright stars in the velvet night, and her kisses were all he needed to tell him the truth. The silken garment was soft under his hands, his body was hard and compelling and his mouth was the song of Solomon, with new passion in the ancient way of a man with a maid.

At last they sat apart, breathless and full of the magic of the place. 'Don't ever leave me,' she begged. 'Take me for ever or go now and leave me here.'

'I nearly lost you,' murmured Tony, taking her close again. 'But I knew I spoke the truth when I said that one day you would look up and find me there.' He kissed the scar that was now hidden by soft hair. 'The past is over and now we have the whole of eternity.' From the desert came the cough of a cat far out in the sand and the silence of the Pharaohs.